Madhulika Liddle is a novelist and award-winning short story writer. Although best known as the author of the Muzaffar Jang series, featuring a 17th century Mughal detective, Madhulika also writes short stories in various genres. Her story, 'A Morning Swim', won the Overall Prize in the Commonwealth Broadcasting Association's Short Story Competition in 2003. In 2016, she became the first Indian to be longlisted for the prestigious *Sunday Times* EFG Short Story Award for her story 'Poppies in the Snow'. In addition, Madhulika blogs about classic cinema, travel, food and history, at www.madhulikaliddle.com.

WOMAN TO WOMAN

Stories

Madhulika Liddle

SPEAKING
TIGER

SPEAKING TIGER PUBLISHING PVT. LTD
4381/4, Ansari Road, Daryaganj
New Delhi 110002

Published in India by Speaking Tiger in paperback 2017

ISBN: 978-93-86702-61-6
eISBN: 978-93-86702-59-3

10 9 8 7 6 5 4 3 2 1

'The Sari Satyagraha' and 'Woman to Woman' were first
published as part of Oxford Bookstore's e-Author version 4.0,
2006; 'Maplewood' was first published in *Open Road
Review*, August 2012; 'Poppies in the Snow' was
longlisted for the *Sunday Times* EFG
Short Story Competition

Typeset in Sabon Roman by SÜRYA, New Delhi
Printed at Thomson Press India Ltd.

For Muriel Liddle and Swapna Dutta,
my mother and her best friend

CONTENTS

Paro

FIVE MINUTES, SANA was to think later. Five minutes, no more. Possibly less. That was all it had taken.

'I'll take Sana with me,' her mother's elder sister had said. 'One week. She'll get to see Guwahati. And she can help with her cousin's wedding.' She had looked out over the green fields and lowering clouds, the shimmering expanse of the Brahmaputra. 'And she will get gifts. Saris and beads, perhaps even gold.'

That had been an eyewash. But to a naïve thirteen-year-old, and to her equally naïve mother, it had sounded irresistible.

'But we'll have to hurry,' her aunt had added. 'We mustn't miss the ferry.'

They had hurried. There had not been much to pack. What would a paddy farmer's daughter—the third in a string of daughters—possess? A pitiful bundle it was, three cotton saris and a pair of earrings of bamboo fibre and wire.

They had been delayed because of the extended farewells: her mother, tearful; her little sisters, envious; her father, back from the fields, incredulous yet relieved. There had been admonitions, warnings, good wishes. Then, just as they were setting out for the ferry, Mariam had come running with the news that their cow had gone into labour.

It was a small matter. Small, yet large. It had delayed them for that vital five minutes, while Sana's mother tried to persuade her husband to go help. Sana's aunt had shifted restlessly. They had dithered, and Sana's father had finally followed Mariam back to her hut, while Sana and her aunt had gone their way.

When they got to the churned mud of the bank, the ferry was nearly mid-river. They would have to go the next day.

The rains came that night. Torrents, crashing and thundering, the wind tearing at the roofs, threatening to blow away everything the water did not sweep away.

They had not slept, not a wink. Not even the littlest of the girls. Instead, they had all huddled together, shivering, praying that the hut would stand fast against the rising waters. Knowing it would not. Sometime during the night, Sana's father had stepped out to see how things were, and had hurried back to urge his family up onto the roof. The river was rising rapidly, its banks already half-submerged. Another hour, and the waters would come rushing, drowning everything in their way.

They had climbed up, taking whatever they could, and waited out the long night on the rickety roof. Dawn had brought little relief, just a scene of horrifying devastation: neighbours up on rooftops, the rain still pouring, drowned cattle floating by.

Relief—or what passed for relief—had begun to arrive by the end of the day, with one lone helicopter whirring overhead, letting down meagre supplies. Another night had gone by, another day had dawned. The rain had lessened, stopped. In the afternoon had come more helicopters, more relief. And Usman Bhai.

He called himself Usman Ali. Or Mohammad Khan. Ram Charan. Whatever was needed. It didn't matter to him, I think, because his only religion was money. Shia, Sunni, Hindu—it was all the same to him, and chameleon-like, he could change himself, his look, his accent, his mannerisms, even that instinctive-seeming touching of a taaveez. Or of his forehead and his lips when he passed a temple. The important thing was that the people he met should believe him. Believe he was of their community, a man to be trusted. A man who truly sympathized with them, felt for them. Could, as he promised, get their daughters married? Here, in this place of devastation? Oh, no, where were the men to marry here? No, he would take the girl to Delhi, far though it was. He had the perfect groom in mind.

Five thousand rupees was the price Usman offered. It was more than Sana's father could imagine. Even without looking at the ruins of his home and his life, he knew he could not say no.

Sana's bundle, already packed, was given over into Usman Bhai's capable hands. So was Sana. Her mother cried. Her sisters were bewildered. Her aunt looked torn between envy and mistrust, but it was not her affair.

The train journey to Delhi was long, tedious. Sana had never been in a train—she had never seen so many people, never been jostled and stared at like this. She huddled against the window, an old woman's bony elbow digging into her ribs on one side, the many bundles and bedrolls of her fellow passengers forcing her to sit with her legs tucked up.

So many years have passed, but I still remember Usman. I remember, too, the man who presided at our wedding. An old man, teeth half-rotted, but invested with the authority

*of solemnizing a marriage. It was done quickly. I remember
the man's eyes, indifferent and dull. I remember another
pair of eyes, large, brown. Eyes that have remained the
same, all these years, though the look in them has changed.*

Delhi overwhelmed Sana, terrified her. Usman took
her to a smelly little house where she was made to sit
while Usman went to fetch her groom. The room was
windowless, its blue-painted walls peeling. Sana wondered
what her husband would be like. Handsome, she hoped.
Perhaps—considering this was Delhi, and everybody knew
people in Delhi were well-off—even rich. Rich enough that
she would not have to work in the fields. Not that Delhi
seemed to have fields.

Her heart leapt when Usman returned. The man who
stepped over the threshold behind him was not bad-
looking. In his mid-twenties, clean-shaven and broad-
shouldered. His grey-eyed gaze swept over her. 'She doesn't
look strong,' he said to Usman when he had finished that
cursory inspection. 'Too thin. And she's dark.'

'What do you expect for ten thousand?' Usman had
snapped back. 'Madhuri Dixit?'

Sana did not know what they were talking about. Who
was Madhuri Dixit? And it wasn't ten thousand, it was five.
She remembered that distinctly. She remembered Usman
handing the money over to her father, her father counting
out each hundred-rupee note.

By the end of the day, she had still not discovered
who Madhuri Dixit was—she never would—but she had
discovered a lot more. The young man was not her groom.
He was merely a go-between, another Usman. The man
he brought, an hour later, and who was married to Sana
that afternoon, was potbellied and thin-limbed. His name

was Basheer. His hair was dyed henna-orange, his mouth dripped paan. He was older than her father.

But he did not treat her like her father did. Not that Sana's father had been a doting man, a devoted father—he had not had the time for that. But he had never been like this. He would never be like this, could not be, thought Sana as she lugged a bucketful of water up the staircase for her husband's bath.

Husband. Yes, husband he was, as he did not hesitate to remind her. As he had emphasized, on that first day, when he had pulled her clothes off and shoved himself into her, heedless of her cries, her shame and confusion. He had left her torn and bleeding, whimpering as she huddled into the evil-smelling sheet. 'I am going out,' he rasped. 'When I get back, I expect to see this place clean and dinner ready.' He spat, leaving a splatter of paan-stained saliva all over the floor. 'Pray that you're a better cook than a cunt, you fool. Otherwise.'

Her cooking did not please Basheer. He sniffed at the pitika, the dish every Assamese mother taught her daughter how to make, before flinging it across the room. 'Boiled potato with mustard oil? Raw mustard oil?' The meat curry he did not comment upon, but he grabbed her hand and pushed it down into the little patila of boiled rice, still steaming. 'Rice? Was that all you could think of? Chappatis, do you hear? I hate rice!'

Her hand blistered, her knees trembling, Sana had crept away, wondering where she would learn how to make chappatis.

Not from the neighbours, who stayed in the other rooms scattered around the shared courtyard of this derelict old haveli. They stared at her with undisguised hostility. She, the outsider. The one who looked different. The one who cooked differently. The one who was alone, rootless and bootless.

A week later, Basheer brought another man home. A burly man, bearded and with streaks of grey in his beard and hair. He looked wordlessly at Sana as she served him tea. When he left, Sana heaved a sigh of relief. There was something unsettling about the man, something even more frightening than the blind raging of her husband.

The next morning, Basheer had sold her off to the man and she was now *his* wife.

Things would have been different if Basheer had realized that treating a new bride the way he did would only lead to misery... I would not be in this condition, lying on this bed, feeling every sagging rope of it digging into my aching body.

A shadow flits by, crossing the doorway. I am not blind yet, nor deaf, though I cannot speak. I shift, making the bed creak. The shadow stops. Turns, approaches. My eldest, Abdul. 'Yes?' he says. Curt, clipped. Too busy doing nothing. Too busy for a crippled parent. This is what I have come to.

Sana did not understand it at first. Not when she was asked if she would accept the other man—his name was Sajid—as her husband. Not when she was made to nod. Not even when she was given ten minutes to gather her belongings. And then Sajid was taking her away, striding through the galis so fast she had to run to keep up. In a local bus, then into a bus depot, stinking of piss, fuel and fumes. Into a ramshackle bus that whisked them away from Delhi. Three hours' drive, four. Through fields, into villages of mud walls and thorn scrub.

Sana felt a surge—a small but definite surge—of relief.

The city had frightened her. The land, though nothing like the moist, verdant countryside of her home, was not the city. This land, even though it was unfamiliar, was like a stranger waiting to be befriended. She alighted from the bus, bruised and burnt from the past week, but hopeful.

That illusion lasted for a day. Not even that. Because Sajid, she found, was not a man to give her time to settle in. He did not care to wait, could not be patient.

He had three brothers, each with his own brood of children. There were hands aplenty to work in the fields and the house. Sajid did not need to go out to work if he was not in the mood to do so. If he felt like it, he could spend all day lolling on his charpai, sucking at his hookah. Drinking chai. Gossiping with passersby.

Or, now that he had a bride, teaching her to be a wife, a slave.

He was brutal. If she did not please him—and she never did—he would hit her, wrap her plait around his arm and pull, while he held her body down with his other hand. There would be curses. Burning beedis stubbed out on her thighs, her tiny girl-breasts. And if his body betrayed him, proving it did find her attractive, there would still be curses. Sana wondered, in a haze of pain and humiliation, why women married if this was what married life was like.

His extended family, all of them inhabiting the same sprawling set of rooms, were no family at all, not to her. 'Paro,' they called her. Not Sana, not bhabhi. Paro. Initially, Sana had been confused. Paro had been the pet name of one of her old childhood friends, Parvati.

'My—my name is Sana,' she finally said one day, while she was helping Sajid's eldest sister-in-law draw water. 'Not Paro.'

The woman was so amused, she let go of the rope. The bucket, heavy with water, went crashing into the depths of the well, carrying the rope with it. Racing through Sana's fingers, leaving a rope burn so fierce it brought tears to her eyes.

'You are a fool,' the woman had said, in an almost awed voice, as if marvelling at Sana's stupidity. 'Don't you know what a paro is? A stolen woman, a bought bride. That's what you are. Little better than a whore. Don't forget it.' And with one vicious tug at the pulley, she had started to haul up the bucket. 'What are you staring at? You're here to work, not gape.'

And work she did. Sweeping and washing, cooking and cleaning. Milking the goats, cutting fodder for the buffalo, doing the million tasks—each more backbreaking, more tedious and filthy than the last—the house and fields entailed. She mended clothes, collected dung and mixed it with chaff to form into thin cakes for fuel. She looked after Sajid's nephews and nieces, and massaged their mothers' legs after lunch, so that the women could have a siesta. She weeded and harvested. She watched Sajid flirt with a passing girl. She tried not to flinch when he saw her watching him and pounced on her. 'Who do you think you're staring at?' She cried when he snatched up the sickle and raked it across her forearm before dragging her to the kitchen to rub salt into the wound.

By the time she was twenty and mother to three children, Sana had stopped crying. Sajid had not stopped hitting her, his relatives had not stopped wounding her in every way they could, but she had hardened. Motherhood had frozen her, down to the core, because she had realized that if her children saw her crying, their distress was too much for her to bear. Their crying also angered Sajid. 'Why is Abdul crying? Can't you keep him quiet? What's wrong with you?'

You. You are the one who has blighted my life, made me what I am today. If I lie in bed, still and useless, my limbs no longer capable of anything, it is because of you. I was wrong when I blamed it on the old man, Basheer—he was just the start of it. I cannot even blame it on Usman, really, who was the first link in the chain. It is all because of you. My helplessness, the anger that gnaws into me. God damn you.

And she had realized she would never go back to the village by the Brahmaputra. For those first few years, even as she sweated and bled her life into the dusty earth of Sajid's village, there had been a glimmer of hope. Some vague dream that one day she would have enough money to buy a train ticket—no, four tickets, for she could not leave her children—to her home.

That dream had faded with time. She had grown up, had realized that it would never happen. When Sajid did not give her enough money even for her to buy a handful of peanuts for the children, when the only clothes he had bought for her in five years was just one salwar-kurta, the rest all cast-offs—how could she hope for money to go home? So she settled in, her body scarred and battered, her being centred on one thing alone: to bring up her children the right way.

I remember the day my sons ganged up on me. The eldest was—what? Thirteen? The youngest not more than eight. Thin, rangy village boys, tough, ruthless. My boys. I had felt pride. This was the way I had wanted my boys to be, not bowing to authority. Fearless.

I had not imagined it would be my authority they would

defy. I had said to the eldest, 'Where are you three off to?
Always running off when you're needed.' I had held out a
hand to the youngest, and he had jerked it away. I had not,
then, thought it serious, so I had merely said, 'Very well.
You two,'—the two younger ones—'Go into the fields and
fetch me six bhuttas. I want the corn nice and ripe, make
sure you don't get me hard kernels. And you, Abdul, go to
Rahim Tau's and tell him I want Rehana to come and press
my legs.'

'Press your legs yourself.'

I had been so infuriated, I had hit out at him with
anything that came to hand. My fists, a shoe, a stick that
stood propped against a nearby wall to chase away dogs.
I opened a gash in his cheek where my ring hit him. I left
bruises on his thin body. I should have killed him.

If I had killed him then, he would not be treating me
like this now.

The day I collapsed on the stairs and came to, only to
find I could not speak or move, I had thought my condition
would make my sons change their minds. That it would be
a reconciliation. After all, a parent is a parent.

I was wrong. And you, Sana, the vile mother of these
vile sons of mine, the perpetrator of these crimes against
your own husband: you are the one who has brought them
up to hate me, their father. I rue the day I bought you from
Basheer. I rue the day Usman told me about you. Paro,
indeed. I gave fifteen thousand for you, and look what you
have brought me. Nothing but pain.

Abdul turns, walks away. I hear his laughter, light and
happy, as he talks to his mother in the courtyard. Sana's
voice is faint, but I can hear the triumph in it. The ease,
the sense of entitlement. She thinks of herself no longer

as my wife, but as the mother of Abdul and Yusuf and Mohammad. And to them, she is the only parent.

I am nothing.

Author's note: An estimated 10 lakh trafficked brides, known as 'paros' or 'molkis', are believed to live in the states surrounding Delhi. Nearly all share stories similar to Sana's.

Ambika, Mother Goddess

AMBIKA HAD BEEN prepared for pain. She had not been prepared for agony.

The spasms squeezed her belly, wringing tears from her eyes and muffled whimpers from her throat. Somewhere, through the blur that surrounded her, she heard the midwife say, 'It will not be long now. She will have to start pushing soon.' Ambika's mother murmured something in reply. Ambika did not hear what. A fresh wave of pain had hit by then.

When it passed and she opened her eyes, the patchy blue-green distemper of the little room looked brighter than before. Someone—the midwife, perhaps—had turned on the single tube light. On the aluminium trunk that doubled as table and dresser were piled old sheets and a torn sari that was not even worth patching any more. Everything that usually stood on the trunk had been moved away: Ambika's comb, her hairpins and plastic bangles, the bottle of hair oil. Only the little painted idol of the goddess Lakshmi with its brass lamp that Ambika's mother had lit just a few minutes ago, still stayed on the trunk. Watching over Ambika. She hoped.

Her mother's hand was on her forehead, wiping away the perspiration. 'Ma,' Ambika groaned. 'How much longer?'

'Soon. Don't worry, we are here.'

Ambika wondered who the *we* meant. Her mother and the midwife, she supposed.

More pain came, the spasms now closer together, and Ambika wished she could pass out. Fall into a faint, slide into a state of peaceful oblivion from which she would emerge a mother. Free of this child that was tearing her apart.

'Think how wonderful it will be to have your own child,' her mother whispered. She had kept up a stream of advice, a litany of dos and don'ts, over the past few months. *Think happy thoughts. Don't eat papayas. Drink a glass of unboiled milk before breakfast, that way, the baby will be born fair and beautiful.* Most of all, *think happy thoughts.*

But all that had come to Ambika's mind was the thought of pain. The pain that was to come, and the pain that had been.

It had been an evening like this, only much colder. That had been January, the heart of Delhi's winter. Cold, so unconquerable, so cruel that no matter how many layers of clothing she donned—and she did not have many—Ambika could not get truly warm, even when she was out in the sunshine. Her hands, chapped from housework, were swollen and dry. Her feet were icy all the time. And the very thought of having to step out of the house after sunset made her shiver.

Her father had been late coming home that evening. Ambika and her mother had been sitting beside the smoking chulha, Ambika making the rotis while her mother chopped onions, when he had appeared in the doorway.

One hand had been clutching the neck of a bottle wrapped in crumpled newspaper. The other wavered and then gripped the doorpost, so hard that his knuckles shone white. The bloodshot eyes bulged slightly and seemed to have difficulty focusing. He had bought one of his thrice-a-week bottles of tharra on his way home from the factory where he worked. And, from the smell and the sight of him, he had consumed a good bit of the stuff on the way home. Perhaps one of the other men had treated him to a glass or two. They did that sometimes. Today, it would be him being treated, tomorrow, he would do the treating. Either way, there was liquor. Every day, without fail.

And sometimes, when he wanted something more, there was also a paan. Laced with tobacco, potent. Perfect with the tharra, he said.

But the paan shop did not lie on the way back from the factory. It stood half a kilometre down the opposite way, past the dingy little grocery store, a barber's shop with one chair, a garbage dump, the stagnant pond—and the mechanic's garage.

It was Ambika's job to go and fetch the paan for her father when he developed a hankering for one. It did not matter if it was raining. Or if the fog outside was more opaque than the water in the pond. She had to go—it was her duty.

That evening, too, she had gone. She had made the last of the rotis, wrapped them in a piece of soft cloth, and pulled down the sleeves of her heavy cardigan. She had borrowed her mother's shawl—maroon, thick and almost blanket-like, shot through with threads of fake gold—because her own cardigan would not be enough. And she had gone out into the night, the ten rupees for the paan clutched in her fist.

Ambika had never made it to the paanwallah's little stall.

Between the garage and the paan shop, she had thought she heard something. Through the fug of cowdung smoke and sewage, a whiff of engine oil had reached her nostrils. Then, just as she had glanced nervously about, an arm had whipped out from around the dark corner of a lane, and pulled her in.

She had writhed, struggled, tried to scream—but he had been too strong for her. One palm, greasy and tasting of engine oil, had clamped down so hard across her mouth that her teeth had bitten into her lips. The other hand had grasped her wrist, twisting her arm behind her while his body had propelled her swiftly backwards until her spine hit a wall.

Ambika did not remember the details. Not then, not later. All she had been aware of throughout was the pain, the terror, the taste of engine oil and blood in her mouth. When he let go, she collapsed on the damp ground, hands shaking, the vomit rushing to her lips. By the time she had thrown up, retched, wiped her mouth and looked around, she was alone in the dark alley.

She had stood up on shaky legs, pulled down her kurta—one seam was ripped—and pulled up her salwar. There had been blood, semen and mud. Lots and lots of mud. Ambika had picked up her mother's shawl and wrapped it around her, grateful in a detached way that it was so big. It would hide the stains when she stepped out into the lane outside.

And it had, well enough to keep her an anonymous feminine figure that hurried down the twisting lane. Not to the paanwallah, but in the opposite direction. Back home.

At the doorway into the small courtyard, she had paused, but only briefly. Instead of going into the house, she had slunk to the back, and into the tiny makeshift toilet.

A plastic bucket full of water, with a mug, was always kept there.

The water had been cold, so icy that she had begun shivering when she splashed herself with it. But it had not stopped her. She had continued. Splashing, scrubbing in a frenzy, sluicing again and again till she felt numb—but still unclean. Then, with her salwar rucked up around her knees, she had leaned her head against the tin sheet that formed the door of the toilet.

At first there had been just tears, trickling silently down her cheeks and falling onto the front of her cardigan. But tears, when there is nobody to wipe them away, have a horrible way of turning into a flood, and with that flood had come sobs. Low sobs, shuddering through her, making her chest ache. Making all of her ache.

'Ambika? Are you in there?' Her mother's voice, on the other side of the tin sheet.

Ambika had not answered. Go away, she had wanted to say. I will not come out, ever. Go away.

'When did you come back? Why didn't you come inside the house?' Her mother's palm had slapped against the tin sheet, making it rattle. Ambika had pulled away—and the sobs had turned into wails.

'Ambika! What's wrong?' There had been worry in her mother's voice, panic.

In her father's voice there had been neither.

He had looked up, surprised and bleary-eyed, when Ambika's mother had led their daughter into the room, one arm clutching Ambika around the shoulders, the other arm holding the shawl so that it hung to below Ambika's knees.

'Where's my paan?' Ambika's father had asked, in a voice slurred with drink. He had waited for a reply, but when both wife and daughter had ignored him, he had called out again, louder this time. Petulant. 'Where is my paan? Don't tell me you dropped the money somewhere!'

Ambika, by then bundled into her charpai at the end of the room, had pulled the quilt up around her head, burrowing deep into its warmth. Trembling, weeping. She had not even known when the murmur of her mother's voice drifted away and she heard her father cry out, *'What!'*

Inside the cocoon of the quilt, Ambika had used everything—the shawl, the quilt, her own muffled sobs—to try and blot out the conversation being held at the other end of the room. They had spoken in low voices, but she had still heard snatches. Her mother, asking in a despairing way, 'But what will we do? What can we do?'

And her father. Agitated and angry and desolate, all at once. 'Why the hell did you let her go out on her own? Can't you see it's dark? Don't you know what it's like outside? *Have you lost your mind?'*

Her mother's silence, accusing.

'She must have been making eyes at him. That's why he did it. I've told you so many times, don't send her out on her own. How did she know who it was, eh? She can even name him! How can she name him if she doesn't already know him?' His voice had risen into a screech, and Ambika had heard every word.

Her mother, defending her daughter. No, Ambika did not know the man. Just knew his name—Kuldeep—because she had heard it called out a few times when she was passing by the mechanic's shop, or when she was waiting at the paanwallah's for the paan to be made.

No, her father had insisted. There had to be fire to create smoke. Why couldn't he have had a son? Why a daughter who would besmirch the name of the family so?

They had gone on talking, arguing long into the night, and Ambika had finally fallen asleep, too exhausted to stay awake any longer. Sometime during the night, she had felt her mother slip into bed beside her. Ambika's eyes had flicked open for the briefest of moments. She had noticed the dim light of the bulb still on, and had guessed that her father was still awake. She had drifted back into sleep. The dawn would bring its own worries.

And it had. Because, during the night, her father had killed himself.

Ambika had woken in the morning to the sound of her mother's screams, and had poked her head out of the quilt to find her parents huddled together at the other end of the room. Her father, slumped and with his chin covered with dried froth. Her mother, clutching him, keening, rocking back and forth until the plastic chair on which he had been sitting keeled over, spilling both of them onto the cold mud floor.

It was rat poison, whispered the neighbours amongst themselves when the news spread. What would push a man to do away with himself like that, all of a sudden? They did not say it out aloud, of course—it was not polite to do so, not with the dead man's body still lying in the house, unwashed and uncremated. But Ambika could sense the gossip working its way through the crowd: as invisible as a spider's newmade web, but as tensile, too. Growing with every passing moment, gathering strength.

The voices had become louder by the next day. Ambika's father was now ashes, and the women of the neighbourhood had come to commiserate. They had jostled their way into every corner of the pokey little home. Some had brought food for the widowed wife and the orphaned daughter.

Some had brought genuine sympathy. The majority had come to see what gossip they could pick up.

There had been those who had heard her father's voice raised that night. They had heard Ambika's weeping, the frenetic pleading of her mother. And there was, after all, the very fact that he had committed suicide.

The secret, ugly and shameful, had come bubbling up, because Ambika's mother had been too weary and too alone to hold on to it any longer. Suddenly, she, Ambika, had become the centre of attention. Their eyes had bored into her, the whispers had all been about her. They had said, first softly and tentatively, then with growing conviction— all the things her father had said. That it was her fault. She must have lured the man on. She had been stupid to venture out all alone on a foggy night.

'No wonder her father killed himself,' someone had said. 'I would have, too, if I had been in his place. Never able to hold up one's head in society again.' It was a man— the men of the area had also started to drift by the house, stopping by to see for themselves what their womenfolk had already whispered to them.

'But what can be done now?'

'Nothing. Forget it. We'll keep quiet.'

'But who will marry her, now?'

There had been no answer to that. After a while, a woman who was a sweeper at the government school in the neighbouring colony had mentioned the police. They had, almost to a man, turned on her. 'Are you out of your mind? The police? That's the best way of spreading the word! Why not put it in the newspapers?'

It had only been much later, after several weeks, that it had become apparent that the episode could not be simply brushed aside as just another unfortunate incident. 'I do not have the money to take her to a hospital,' Ambika's mother had said, flat-voiced and stony-faced, to the elders who had congregated in her house in response to her summons. Somebody had whispered something about the midwife knowing ways of ridding a woman of an unwanted child. Ambika's mother had shaken her head at that. She had been suddenly, irrationally, adamant. No. Ambika would not be subjected to the midwife's quack remedies. What if something should happen? What if—she only had Ambika now. Only Ambika to look after her in her old age.

They had tried to reason with her. Words like *reputation* and *izzat* had been tossed about. Ambika, her head bowed, had crouched in the tiny shed that served as kitchen, and heard it all. But her mother had remained steadfast. She would not agree to what they suggested.

'Then,' an old man had said—he was the oldest in the community, his white hair brittle as straw and his jaws close to toothless—'there is only one thing to be done. We will speak to Kuldeep.'

***

The midwife was saying something in a hurried, raised voice. Ambika's mother's hands were on her daughter's shoulders. Holding her down? Or supporting her? Ambika could not tell, and did not care. All she wanted was for the pain to go. But it did not. Instead, it burgeoned, building up until she thought the child would rip her apart in its attempts to break free. She was screaming now, her ragged cries drowning out even the urgent 'Push! Push!' of the midwife. She was clinging to the sides of the charpai, feeling the ropes of it bite through the thin mattress and into her bony hips.

When she finally drifted into a consciousness of what was happening around her, Ambika found the baby—small and wrinkled and red-faced—wrapped in an old sheet, burrowing into her side. She had been cleaned, she could sense that much, but the pain was still there. It felt as if it would never leave her. She would go to her funeral pyre with her body still throbbing.

'Jamaaiji,' Ambika heard her mother say. *Son-in-law, sir.* The deference was there not just in the way she addressed him, but in her voice too. The words were almost hushed. Awe? Or, as Ambika suspected, fear? Fear of the man who held her daughter's future—and, by extension, her own—in his hands? Ambika closed her eyes. Even her eyelids hurt.

'Look, jamaaiji,' her mother was saying, 'look, what a lovely little daughter you have.' Ambika was dimly aware of her mother coming to her bedside, reaching out to lift the fragile bundle from beside her. 'Isn't she a beauty?' There was a clear thread of anxiety running through those words.

'Hmm.' Her husband must have entered the room. Ambika could smell the engine oil. It made her want to throw up. She heard his feet dragging on the floor. Then his voice, angry, accusing. 'A girl. A blasted *girl*. What good is your daughter, eh?' There was silence, the guilty silence of her mother and the hostile silence of her husband. She heard him clear his throat and spit. 'I'm going now.'

And that was it. Her mother put the baby back beside Ambika, cooing for a brief moment. She was gone the next, following her son-in-law across the threshold. Outside, the midwife was waiting to be paid. Ambika heard her mother begin to haggle with the woman. *They were a poor family.*

She was a widow. The only man to support them was her son-in-law, and—there was an uncomfortable silence, the speaker too embarrassed to say more, the listener not needing to be told.

Everybody around here knew. Kuldeep had been threatened by the community elders: they would let him stay on, let him run that little mechanic's shop of his and not turn him out, only if he married the girl he had got with child. Kuldeep, sullen even when confronted by the elders, had held his own. All right, all right. He would marry the little bitch. But he would not look after her or her mother. They would stay on in their own house. They would provide for themselves. His name, that was all Ambika would get.

'What about the child?' the sarpanch had asked. 'The child will be yours. You will have to pay for its upkeep.'

Kuldeep had conceded, reluctantly, that he would. But that had come with a qualifier: if the child was a boy. A boy, he would look after. A girl would be better off drowned, or thrown into a ditch somewhere. He had not said that in so many words, but Ambika knew. A son would be useful, a daughter a burden.

This one seemed like no burden at all. She was so small, so light. So helpless.

Ambika opened her eyes and gazed down at her child. The baby looked up, eyes now wide in a wrinkled face. Staring solemnly up at her mother, as if recognizing her. Ambika put her arm around her daughter, gently tugging the baby closer, trying to press a kiss to the downy head—but even that little effort made her ache, so she contented herself with simply caressing the soft cheek with her fingertip. One small arm reached up. A tiny fist curled around her finger.

A tear rolled down Ambika's cheek and sank into the

pillow. 'Grow up soon,' she mumbled. 'Please? Grow up soon, so we can be friends.' With her free hand, she wiped away the tears from her own face, but there were more, coming swiftly in a flood she could not stem.

'After all,' she whispered, 'thirteen years isn't much of a gap.'

Mala

ASHU TURNED THREE that April. Sushil's parents phoned to wish their only grandchild, and spent a minute cooing at him before Ashu got bored and ran off.

'Send him to us this summer,' Sushil's mother said, when Sushil took the phone. 'A couple of years now and he'll be going to school. Then he won't want to spend any time with his old grandparents.' She let that sink in before launching another attack from the formidable arsenal of emotional artillery she commanded so well. 'Who knows if we will even be around to see Ashu's next birthday? Our only grandchild, and so far away.'

Sushil's company was singularly stingy when it came to granting leave. Three days, and that was it. Just enough to take Vandana and Ashu to his parents', spend a day there, and come back. Vandana had over a month's leave due to her, but she cribbed about going nevertheless. She had little in common with her in-laws, and without even Sushil to keep her company, she dreaded the two weeks she had promised to spend, along with Ashu, at their house.

The train ride, even though it was in an air-conditioned compartment, was harrowing. Ashu's excited fascination with everything around—the dull blue fake leather of the seats, the large red suitcase of the woman in the berth opposite, the lights twinkling in the towns and villages through which the train journeyed, the repetitive rub-dub-dub, rub-dub-dub of the train itself, even the sight of a coolie wearing his uniform of a long red shirt over a white dhoti—lasted only till midnight. Then, inevitably, the excitement crumbled, leaving behind a very tired, very sleepy and cranky three-year-old who howled till his father was forced to carry him out into the secluded little passage near the toilets. It was not pleasant, but at least there was nobody around to glare at them there.

They arrived late in the morning. Ashu had not regained his good temper. It was hot and dusty on the small platform, where they had to wait while Sushil haggled with a rickshawwallah to pedal them home. There were flies, and Ashu was hungry.

Home was a large two-storeyed house, built around a paved courtyard. A lush green mango orchard surrounded three sides of the house. Sushil's parents and their neighbours and two of the men who worked in the orchard were there, standing in the veranda, smiles plastered across their faces. Sushil's father was all bluff good humour, wishing his daughter-in-law many years of married life and hugging his grandson until Ashu burst out crying all over again. Sushil's mother, after a somewhat more restrained greeting—at least as far as Vandana was concerned—led the way in.

A girl, not yet twenty, emerged from the kitchen, bearing a small plastic tray with half a dozen glasses full of cold water. She showed the tray around in a carefully practised sequence: the elder guests first (the neighbours), the younger guests next (Sushil and Vandana), the hosts last. She was a striking girl. Not tall and not very beautiful, but with a certain something about her that stayed with you long after she had gone, long after you had even forgotten what she really looked like. A generous figure, voluptuous and curvy, eyes that laughed even when her lips weren't smiling and hair that dangled in a long fat plait down her back, past her hips. Ashu, clutching his mother's sari, reached out a hand tentatively and stroked the girl's plait as it swung, glossy and black, just above his face.

The girl looked down, her mouth curving into a friendly smile, a dimple appearing in her cheek. 'Hello.'

Sushil's mother, talking to the lady from next door, turned to look at the girl with hard, cold eyes. 'Mala,' she said in a clipped voice, all admonition, 'Tea.' The girl tapped Ashu's chubby cheek with the tip of her forefinger, freed her plait from his grasp, and went her way.

She was back ten minutes later, the tray now bearing sunflower-printed china mugs of tea. Hot, sweet, milky tea brewed long with peppercorns, cinnamon, cardamom and slices of fresh ginger. She served the tea and then setting the tray down on the table, sat down on her haunches in front of Ashu. 'And what would *you* like to have, my little prince?' she murmured, her dimple twinkling in her cheek like a star. Ashu watched her intently from beside his mother, one fist clenched around a fold of Vandana's sari, then reached forward hesitantly to touch the girl's plait. She laughed, and in one fluid movement, gathered him up in her arms and stood up, resting him easily on her hip. 'Do you like juice, my little prince? Mausambi juice? Yes? Come on, then, we'll go and get you some.'

Ashu favoured her with a small, shy smile and she giggled throatily at him as she carried him off into her domain.

From that moment on, Ashu was inseparable from Mala. She it was who introduced him to the sweet-sour freshness of newly squeezed mausambi juice, from the wicker basket of green-skinned citrus fruit that sat on the kitchen counter. She it was who won him over with just one meal of fluffy puffed rice, cooked with sautéed onions and boiled potatoes and dotted with juicy green peas. 'Have one spoonful of this,' Mala said, squeezing a lime wedge over the poha, the puffed rice, 'and you'll forget all about those potato chips you like so much.' He didn't, of course, potato chips are too ambrosial, at age three, for even the best-cooked poha to supplant them. But Ashu did concede that there was more to life than potato chips.

There was, for instance, Mala's delicious phirni, ground rice simmered very slowly and very long in creamy milk ('Full cream!' gasped Vandana, in horror. 'Not skimmed, let alone double-toned like we buy in Delhi!'). There were fat, satisfying parathas, stuffed with gently spiced potatoes and smeared with ghee. And tall glasses of thick yoghurt whisked with sugar into a froth that left a neat white moustache on Ashu's upper lip—a moustache fit to rival his grandfather's, who laughed uproariously as he compared moochhes with the toddler.

And Mala kept him close at hand. On a small wickerwork stool at a safe distance from her—not close enough to get hurt, not far enough to be out of reach—as she chopped and sliced, ground chunks of ginger and tiny slivers of garlic into pungent pastes on the heavy grinding-stone, and cooked. And all through it, Mala would be chattering away, telling Ashu all the stories she knew.

Briskly stirring the gravy, she would look over her shoulder to where Ashu sat, a plastic quarter-plate cradled in his lap, eating a biscuit. 'Now how far had I got with the story of the monkey and the crocodile?'

Ashu, mouth full of biscuit, would think. Crumbs would erupt, spraying the floor, when he replied triumphantly: 'The monkey gave the crocodile fruit from the jaamun tree to eat.'

'Yes!' Mala would say, peering into the pan to check on the gravy while she washed the rice, again and again and again, until the water ran clear. 'They were lovely, luscious jaamuns. Have you ever had jaamuns, my little prince?' And when Ashu would shake his head, she would describe the jaamuns to him, the way only Mala could, enticing him with word-pictures of the purple-black fruit, astringent and sweet and sour all at once, plump and juicy and oh so wonderful. 'And the jaamuns were so, *so* good that the crocodile's wife, when she ate them, thought: "If the jaamuns are so sweet, how much sweeter will be the heart of the monkey who eats only these jaamuns?"'

Ashu, biscuit forgotten, would stare at her wide-eyed, waiting for the next bit of the story to unfold.

Mala told him many stories, of magical lands peopled by powerful kings and beautiful queens, of apsaras and demons, of talking animals and wily birds. One morning Ashu was shown—with the help of a hot, ghee-laden roti sprinkled over with soft moist brown sugar—how a cunning monkey swindled two cats out of their meal when they went to him for arbitration. Another afternoon, with a small plate of fragrant khichri as a prop, Mala told him of Birbal's sly attempt to cook khichri in a pot hung far away from the fire.

'I like the stories of the kings best,' Ashu said as she fed him a spoonful of the khichri. Then, without giving her time to answer, 'Why do you call me little prince?'

Mala smiled affectionately. 'Because you are my little prince, aren't you? You're handsome and good and strong, just like a prince should be.'

'But that's what you said about kings too. Why can't I be a king?'

Mala's smile softened, and the twinkle in her eyes changed to something Ashu wouldn't have understood even if he had noticed it. She tweaked the child's plump cheek, and murmured, 'Ah, but there is a king already. Some day I'll introduce you to him.'

Three days later, Ashu and Mala returned from a rewarding trip to the local market (where Ashu was introduced to the joys of syrupy squiggly jalebis) to find that a man had arrived. 'Ashu, come and say hello to your Uncle Sudhir,' Vandana said, pulling Ashu out of Mala's arms and giving his cowlick a perfunctory pat. Ashu hadn't the faintest idea of what an uncle was supposed to be. He was also more interested in rushing off after Mala than in saying hello to the strange young man. But he had learnt that mothers could not be thwarted, so he obeyed.

Sudhir smiled, half-distracted, half-affectionate, at Ashu's retreating figure. 'I'll get myself a glass of water,' he said, after a moment, rising to his feet. He noticed the objection in his mother's expression—the 'but there is a servant to bring it for you'—and added, 'It'll give me a chance to stretch my legs too. Driving five hours non-stop is no joke. And certainly not on roads like this, all potholes and dirt.' He bestowed a dazzling smile on his parents and wandered off towards the kitchen. Ashu was there already, the childish high-pitched voice drifting out from the kitchen along with the aromas of ghee and spices and that elusive allure that was Mala.

When Sudhir stepped over the threshold and into the kitchen, Mala was grating a coconut. Ashu, seated on a small wickerwork stool, was nibbling at a strip of coconut and saying, 'But what is an uncle? Do you have an uncle too, Mala?'

Mala glanced over her shoulder at the man whose entry had briefly blotted out the light filtering in through the doorway. Her eyes softened, a smile hovered on her lips, and for the moment, the child was forgotten. Ashu looked on, too shy to speak in the presence of the man. But the man—the uncle—came over to where Ashu was sitting, and lowered himself to the floor, sitting on his heels so that he was looking into Ashu's face. 'An uncle is a friend, Ashu,' he said, with a twinkle in his eyes. 'Just like Mala is your friend. So your uncle can also be your friend. Yes?'

Ashu was not quite sure what that meant. But association with grownups who demanded obedience, if nothing else, had imprinted one important lesson in Ashu's brain. He nodded, eyes wide and watchful. The uncle grinned—he looked a lot like Papa when he smiled, thought Ashu—and then he got to his feet and strolled across the kitchen to where Mala was grating the coconut. He filched a strip of the fruit from her and chewed on it while he watched her, his eyes hooded, the avuncular grin gone, dissolved into an expression of sheer wanting.

'And how are you, Mala?' His voice was low, so low that over the rhythmic khash-khash-khash of Mala's hands working the grater, his words could hardly be heard. But Mala heard them, looked up momentarily and shrugged. 'The same.'

A forefinger played with a long, loose tendril of hair that curled down the side of her face. He curled it around his fingertip, again and again, then let go, watching it remain twined into a ringlet, bouncing against her cheek. The finger trailed down her cheek and settled near her mouth. 'Show us your dimples, Mala.'

She did, involuntarily flattered by the desire brimming in his voice. The next moment, the fear returned. 'Not here. Not in front of the child, please.'

'I've been aching for you,' he murmured. 'Do you know how many days it's been? I've waited all this while to come back to you, and you—' the lover turned petulant.

'Not here,' she insisted stubbornly.

'Then where?'

She told him.

Even though Ashu did not get to know, till he was older, what an uncle implied, he got to see a lot of the young man who had been introduced to him as his uncle. Sudhir would wake up early—much earlier than his parents, much earlier than Ashu's late-sleeping mother Vandana, earlier even than Ashu himself, who awoke punctually at seven and toddled off immediately kitchenwards. He had learnt early on that the kitchen in the early morning was a place of warm, frothy milk and thick lassi, of rich parathas and perhaps a story to accompany the eating of them. A good place to spend the morning in, the kitchen. A place for comfort and happiness and affection.

This first morning after the arrival of the uncle, Ashu stumbled across the threshold of the kitchen, rubbing the sleep from his eyes, to see emptiness. Mala, swinging plait and liberal dimples, was missing from her usual station before the stove. The signs of her recent presence were all there, though. The vegetables chopped and stacked in neat piles, ready to be cooked. The recycled jam jars full of turmeric and red chillies and powdered coriander seeds, all lined up for easy access. The neat taut roll of wholewheat dough, waiting to be rolled into parathas.

Off to the left, a low wall separated the kitchen from the area where pots and pans were scrubbed and washed. The faint clang of a cast iron griddle hitting a steel ladle drifted from beyond the wall. Ashu perked up. He knew this game. 'Mala didi! I know where you are! I'm coming!'

'No! Ashu, no! Don't come here!' But, of course, she was too late. Her buttons were mostly undone, her plait all in loose strands falling to her shoulders. But she managed to push the man back into the shelter of the low wall—'Ashu, my little prince, did I not tell you, you *must* obey?'

Ashu's eyes, huge with curiosity, were looking not at the girl, trying to cover herself with her dupatta, but at the man behind her. The uncle was shrugging on his shirt as he stepped out. 'You're up early, Ashu,' he said. 'Too early.'

Ashu did not reply, instead, he said to Mala, 'I'm hungry. What's there to eat?' He followed her to the kitchen counter and watched as she began working, lighting the stove, sloshing the oil into the pan, tearing off bits of dough and rolling them between her palms. She looked up, past Ashu, towards the uncle. She was smiling, and so was the uncle. Smiling in a way that excluded Ashu, smiling secretly, surreptitiously.

That was how it remained. When his grandparents and mother were out, or when they were asleep—late in the afternoon, or early in the morning—Mala vanished too. Ashu would see her going off into the mango grove surrounding the house, a generous-bosomed figure, her plait swaying in time to her hips, a lilting tune on her lips. She would be gone for an hour, or more—time that had, before the coming of the uncle, been devoted to Ashu. She was still his designated playmate and storyteller and babysitter rolled into one. The kitchen, through much of the day, was still Mala's domain, where she chatted with Ashu, telling him stories while she went about her work. But let the uncle take one step across the threshold of the kitchen, and Mala would lose the thread of what she had been saying.

'You like him,' Ashu said, grumpily perceptive. And then, with a hint of worry in his voice: 'Do you call him *little prince*, too?'

Mala, pouring milk into a glass for Ashu, blew him a kiss. 'No, little prince. He is the king, no? Why will I call him *little prince*?'

'How do you know he's the king? He doesn't wear a crown. Or jewels.'

She stirred drinking chocolate briskly into the milk. 'He's a king in disguise. The crown and the jewels stay hidden away. But you've seen how handsome he is, how strong and handsome and wonderful. That's what a king is all about. He's a king, all right.'

Two days later, the king brought home a queen.

A phone call had come that morning for Sudhir, and he had been on the phone for nearly half an hour before ringing off. He had gone out into the veranda for a while, pacing up and down its length, gazing out into the mango trees. And then he had gone into the room where his father was reading the newspaper and his mother was darning socks. Sudhir had said, 'I have to speak to both of you,' and without giving them time to react, had firmly shut the door behind him, locking the three of them into the room for the next couple of hours.

Mala, who had taken Ashu along with her to the grocer's for shopping, came back with her arms loaded down with purchases, Ashu sucking a lollipop as he walked in beside her. Vandana, sitting on the veranda with a magazine, looked up and scowled. 'Don't give him those vile things to suck,' she said. 'Here, Ashu—spit that thing out.'

Ashu did not listen to her, and Mala's only reaction was to lower the bulging plastic bags to the floor. 'They didn't have the shampoo you wanted, didi,' she said. 'Where is maaji? I have to show her the scrubber I got'—she unearthed a bright red pad of plastic wire, which looked flimsy and gaudy. 'They didn't have any steel wool, so we'll have to make do with this for now.' She glanced up, frowning, as the sound of raised voices filtering through the closed door caught her attention. Her head turned, eyes narrowed with curiosity, looking to Vandana for an answer.

Vandana looked, deadpan, back at Mala. 'I'm sure the plastic wool will do,' she said. 'Go to the kitchen, Mala; your work is waiting.'

So Mala was in the kitchen, stirring the lentils, when the door finally opened and Sudhir emerged. On his heels came his mother, eyes red and swollen, seeking out Vandana to pour out all her woes. The wicked, wicked boy—no respect for the wishes of his parents—now he tells us he's been married these past seven months. Eloped, and with a girl we've never even met—now she's pregnant, and they think it's time she came and met us. Hey Ram, what had the world come to? To think that her very own son, the son whom she had brought up to be such a good boy, should deceive them so horribly. And now they would have to be grandparents to a child of God knows what parentage—it was too frightful to contemplate.

Sudhir left in his car fifteen minutes later. The rest of the day passed in a welter of emotions: Sudhir's parents felt put upon, indignant and worthy of much pity. Vandana was excited—this was a godsend, an unforeseen bit of adventure in what had looked to be a boring fortnight at her in-laws'. Ashu and Mala, both aware that something was wrong, but both—one unconcerned and the other not bold enough to ask—remained silent.

Late the next day, at a time when the old people would have been sleeping away their lunch, the car drew up at the gate. Sudhir climbed out, and the young woman sitting next to him slid into the driver's seat. She waited for him to open the gate, then drove the car in, stopping briefly just inside the gate for Sudhir to get back in. Her voice, tinkling laughter and clipped English, floated on the wind.

From the mango orchard, attracted by the unfamiliar sounds of car engine and English, came the only two members of the household who were abroad. Mala had taken Ashu with her into the depths of the mango grove. She had been up a tree, shaking the branches and letting the raw green baby mangoes shower onto the sheets she had spread underneath. Ashu had been given the task of picking up any mangoes that fell outside the pale. The arrival of Sudhir had accelerated the harvesting of the mangoes. Mala had hurriedly shinned down the tree and gathered up the corners of the sheets, knotting them into bundles and slinging them over her shoulder.

'It's uncle, isn't it, Mala didi?' Ashu asked, breathlessly, as they ran, hand in hand, towards the front veranda.

Mala, red-faced and panting, arrived just as Vandana and her mother-in-law emerged from the house. Just as Sudhir opened the car door for the woman, slim and fashionable and exquisite, who had driven the car into the driveway. Just as Sudhir said, 'Ma, this is Shaila.' Just as Shaila bent, for all the world like a traditional Hindu daughter-in-law, her fingertips brushing her mother-in-law's toes in a gesture of ceremonial esteem. Just as Sudhir's mother nodded, her eyes glassy and expressionless, her lower lip jutting disapprovingly.

The bundle slung over Mala's left shoulder came undone. Mangoes spilled in a shower of green, thudding and bouncing off the ground, rolling under the car, setting off a wave of mirth as Ashu raced after the fruit, giggling. Mala stood, her right hand clutching the other bundle. Sudhir's father, who had now come out of the house and was being introduced to Shaila, glanced at Ashu gathering up the mangoes and placing them neatly on the edge of the veranda. 'Mala,' he said, 'Water.'

'And tea,' Sudhir's mother added as Mala went past her and into the house. Mala did not nod her head or say yes.

They went in, eventually, this family that had so suddenly acquired a new member. A new member who was unwelcome and unnecessary, but whom they, out of a sense of politeness, felt called upon to welcome. To be kind and courteous towards, even if they wished Shaila had brightened the threshold of some other home. That their son should have been so forward. It was shameful.

'Where on earth is that girl?' Sudhir's mother whispered to Vandana. 'No water, no tea, nothing. Where has she taken herself off to?'

'We'll go and look for her,' Vandana offered, eager to escape the suffocating politeness of the room. 'Come, Ashu, we'll go find your Mala didi, shall we?'

She was not in the kitchen, though she had brewed

the tea and left it in the squat aluminium kettle on the counter next to the cups. She was not in that little section, partitioned off with the low wall, where Ashu had once found her. She was not in any of the other rooms, and not in the little outhouse abutting the courtyard, where the empty flowerpots and the sacks of manure were stored along with the odds and ends used to tend the mango trees. She was not even up in the loft where the old suitcases were stacked.

'Perhaps she's in the orchard,' Vandana murmured, and mother and child went out into the grove, Ashu wandering off to the left of the house, Vandana to the right.

It was just as well, said Vandana later, that she had been on her own when she found Mala. The sight of that figure, dangling marionette-like from the branch of one of the older trees, was enough to shake up Vandana pretty badly too. Poor Ashu would have been traumatized. As it happened, all he was told while Mala was discreetly removed from the scene was that Mala didi had gone away and would never come back.

'Why? Did the king take her away?' Ashu asked. Then, as his gaze fell on Sudhir, standing there, one arm draped possessively around Shaila's shoulders, he shook his head. 'But he's still here.'

Vandana and her mother-in-law looked at each other, puzzled. 'I don't know,' Vandana said, finally. 'She used to tell him all sorts of stories. This was one of them, I suppose.'

Sudhir's mother shrugged. 'I suppose.' She made a face. 'Stupid girl, going and killing herself just now, when the house is full of people. How am I to cook for everybody all by myself?' She sighed, the very picture of long-suffering martyrdom. 'I suppose I should be grateful that she at least made tea before she went and hanged herself. Do you want some tea? I'll heat it up again.'

But the tea, when Sudhir's mother had a look at it, was not enough for all of them. It was barely enough for one person. And it was not the type of tea she, or her husband, or even Vandana, liked. There was no milk to speak of, no cardamoms, no cinnamon, not a trace of ginger or tulsi or anything to make it interesting.

'Sudhir,' she called out. 'She's made plain tea, the way you like it. Do you want some? There's enough for you.'

Everybody knew that was the way Sudhir liked his tea. Plain, with just a drop of milk added. And a little sugar.

'What an idiot,' his mother muttered, as she poured it out in a mug for him. 'Why did she make this tea? Nobody but you has this.' Sudhir looked uncomfortable, but said nothing. He took the tea, and went off to sit in the veranda while he drank it. He had swallowed half of it before he began complaining of a strange burning in his throat. The nausea and the giddiness came on soon after, and by the time the old people and Shaila panicked and sent for the doctor, he was already unconscious. The doctor arrived to find a corpse. Ashu and Vandana returned from the park shortly after, and Ashu was told that the uncle had gone. Gone, never to return.

'Hmm,' Ashu said, when it was gently explained to him by Vandana that his uncle had gone. 'Mala didi went, no? She took him with her, no? I thought she wouldn't have gone alone.'

Woman to Woman

THE ROAD MEANDERED up from the dusty plains into the green foothills, which were cloaked, even at noon, with a shifting mist. Dense groves of fragrant cardamom and scented cinnamon, pungent pepper and the aromatic twin spices of nutmeg and mace—all lay smothered by the mist, which wove its translucent tendrils through the deep pile of tea bushes carpeting the higher slopes, snaked over bubbling streams, and blanketed the pools at the foot of each waterfall.

The mist even pushed its way in through the windows of the bus, borne on a breeze that must have been a blessing to those who sat within. But neither the mist nor the scented breeze did anything to rouse the passengers from the somnolent state into which nearly all had drifted. This was a well-traversed route for many of them, and its beauties too familiar to invite comment. Also, the bus had begun its journey shortly before dawn, and all passengers had been forced to rise at an unearthly hour. They were now catching up on some much-needed sleep, and minor disturbances— such as the incessant honking of an impatient car—drew no more than an indignant wail from a sleepy toddler or a muttered curse from one of the men sitting at the front of the bus.

Film music blaring from a roadside eatery, the shrill cries of hawkers at a hill village, the frenzied yapping of pariah dogs chasing the bus: none could waken the rickety vehicle's slumbering inmates for more than a minute or two.

It was, therefore, not surprising that the two-minute halt at an obscure village went almost unnoticed. A handful of people on board realized that the bus had stopped, but they too, after reassuring themselves that their own destinations lay far away, dozed off again. A couple of passengers noticed that a single person boarded the bus, but that was all. There was the usual buying of the ticket from the sleepy conductor, the driver's customary yell—to nobody in particular—that the bus was continuing, and then the lurch forward.

The new passenger, in fact, may have drawn a few curious glances had those in the bus been more awake. She was a nun, perhaps in her early thirties. A dark grey habit, reaching down to stocking-clad calves, hid a slender figure, and the face framed by a severe white wimple was a tranquil, attractive one. Had her attire not proclaimed her celibacy, had her co-passengers not been dozing peacefully, she may certainly have been an object of admiration for many.

A shapeless bag, woven from coir, hung from the nun's right shoulder as she stood near the conductor's seat, searching the bus with worried brown eyes for a place to sit. A single look around the bus was enough to convince her that all the possible places were taken. Most of the seats were occupied by families. Mothers clad in rumpled cotton saris, wilted flowers encircling their plaits, leaned drowsily against the bars of windows, clinging to babies who dozed, open-mouthed, on their bosoms. Older children sat wedged against their mothers, sleeping against a dependable arm. Fathers balanced on the edges of narrow seats, trying to grab forty winks while keeping a hold on the back of the seat in front.

Towards the front of the bus, half a dozen seats were occupied by a group of teenaged boys in school uniforms. Beyond them sat a few men, perched rather precariously, but asleep nevertheless.

Those boys may have been chivalrous enough to give her a seat, perhaps, or maybe one of the men on board with their families. If they had been awake.

But nobody was awake.

The nun, one arm wrapped around the pole next to the door, looked around unhappily.

It was then that she spotted a vacant seat. It was right at the back, and there was space on it for only one more person. A two-seater bench, with a woman next to the window. And an empty space next to her.

Thank you, Lord.

The nun offered up a silent word of gratitude, and lurched her way towards the vacant seat.

The woman on the bench was awake. Like the other women, she was dressed in a cotton sari, but there the resemblance ended. Where her co-passengers were matronly, this one was almost glamorous. Her cotton sari was edged with gold, and was—God alone knew how she had managed it—still crisp with starch. The jasmine flowers entwined in the thick plait were fragrant and fresh, and the jewellery was obviously of pure gold, worked by an expert craftsman.

Her hands were smooth and well kept, the nails shaped and painted, not blunted by years of washing utensils and scrubbing floors. The face was not exceptionally beautiful, but kohl, lipstick and rouge—all applied with a lavish hand—made it more striking than it actually was.

The nun, now within arm's length of the woman, looked at her with the faintest of misgivings. This woman looked strange. Not ordinary. Surely there was something wrong?

But no. Her faith had taught her to judge no man. Or woman. She would not pass judgement on one of whom she knew nothing.

The nun stepped forward, a hesitant smile on her attractive face.

'Could I sit down?' Her voice was soft and mellifluous, almost as gentle as the breeze that whirled soothingly in from the open window next to the woman, who sat looking up at the nun. On her face was an inscrutable expression, the nun could not quite tell what. Perhaps bitterness, perhaps sorrow, perhaps even irony—definitely something that was unpleasant—but with a tinge of amusement.

For what seemed well over a minute, the woman said nothing. She sat there quietly, her hands in her lap, staring up at the nun. Then, when the nun had just about begun to wonder whether the woman was perhaps deaf, she spoke.

'Of course you *could* sit,' she replied, in a low, slightly harsh voice—like the invisible splinters that mar the edge of an otherwise smooth surface. 'Of course you could sit but would you want to?'

The nun stared back, perplexed and uncomfortable. There was something horrendously wrong here, she realized—but it would be rude to turn around and sneak away to another seat—no, but there was nowhere to sit in the bus anyway. She had no choice.

'I don't understand,' she murmured unhappily—and untruthfully.

'Can you not guess why nobody sits here?' asked the woman, her reddened lips curving into a sardonic smile. 'Why is it that every other seat on the bus is taken—that two sit where only one may comfortably fit? Why is it that no one will sit in this empty seat?'

The nun remained silent. One hand still clung to the coir bag, the other gripped the backrest of a neighbouring seat.

'I,' said the woman, in a voice that was proud in its sheer audacity, 'am a fallen woman. A prostitute, a whore, a woman of the street, call me what you will. Not one with whom anybody decent—least of all one like you—would wish to come in contact.'

There was a dull silence, relieved only by the rattling of the bus.

'You see,' continued the woman, as if she was making conversation beside a village well rather than in a shuddering bus, and that too to one who looked most reluctant to enter into a conversation. 'You see, my very profession is such that though I may bathe oftener than anybody in this bus and though I may be a hell of a lot cleaner than any of them, yet I am tainted. Tainted beyond redemption, an object of contempt. They all recognized me as soon as they saw me, even though I wear no badge of my trade, no outward sign, like you do—yet they knew me. As you did.'

The nun squirmed, wishing to put an end to this unpleasant talk. All she could think of was to say, in her quiet voice, 'May I sit?'

The woman blinked at her, then after a moment's pause, she nodded.

Still clinging carefully to her bag, the nun sat down next to the woman, who shifted a little to make place for her. There was silence for a few moments, while the nun made herself as comfortable as she could on the hard, unyielding wood of the bench. When she looked up, it was to see the woman regarding her with curiosity. The nun looked away, uncomfortable and tongue-tied. Her face was by now red with embarrassment, and it was obvious that she was not enjoying the fact that fate had dumped her next to a companion such as this.

The prostitute watched the nun in silence for some time but her silence was, rather than the apprehension of the nun, a sardonic and even contemptuous contemplation of the one who sat beside her. Her large, keen eyes gazed out from under eyelids heavily painted over with glittering eye shadow—and that gaze was intense enough to disconcert the nun, who began to fumble with her bag.

More than a minute passed, and then the woman spoke. Her tone was conversational enough, but what she said made the nun's head jerk up in shock.

'You needn't cringe so. I'm not going to molest you, you know.'

The nun stared, wild-eyed, at the prostitute, seeking in that heavily made-up face some reason for this seemingly unreasonable assault.

It was the prostitute who spoke again, and not the nun. 'Really,' she scolded. 'You should be more sociable. After all, you and I probably have a lot more in common than you imagine.'

The nun's disturbed gaze met the mirthless smile in her co-passenger's eyes. Then, as if realizing that what could not be cured must perforce be endured, the nun spoke. 'Something in common? Between you and me?' The words were barely audible.

'Why not? Think about it.' The woman toyed with the

bangles she wore on her wrist, jangling them absently as she spoke. 'Your calling is one that not too many venture into, so is mine. You live in the company of women, separated from the mundane realities of family existence, so do I. You are celibate, so am I—'

She was interrupted, for the first time, by a sudden flash of spirit on the part of the nun. The tranquillity of her face was marred momentarily by what could only be termed indignation. 'Celibate?' she retorted. 'How can you even talk of celibacy?'

It was the prostitute's turn to interrupt, and she did so with a harsh, unattractive burst of laughter. 'Why? Do you mean to tell me you aren't celibate?'

The utter dismay on the face of the nun, who was too shocked to even respond to this taunt, seemed to calm the prostitute. She replied in a quieter voice, 'No, of course that's not what you meant. What you meant was that I couldn't possibly know anything of celibacy. Isn't that so?'

The answer was an embarrassed silence, a lowering of lashes over flushed cheeks.

'But strangely enough, I am celibate—in a way. Do you know,' she murmured as she glanced out of the window, staring unseeingly at the green-clad hills beyond, 'my body is touched, but never *me*. I have given pleasure to countless men—but not one has reached into the most intimate parts of my being. Not one has made the slightest impression on what I call my true self.'

There was silence for a while—a silence that was contemplative on the part of the whore, and shocked on the part of the nun. After a few minutes had passed, the prostitute asked abruptly, 'You ever been in love?'

To her own surprise, the nun nodded slowly. Her voice,

when she spoke, was hoarse and tinged with guilt. 'When I was fifteen,' she whispered.

The other woman looked thoughtful, but did not say anything, and it was after a while that the nun continued. 'My family was a large one, and we were not well off. My parents could not afford to get me married.'

'So you became a nun?' There was a sudden kindness in her voice, a sympathy that had not been there before.

The nun was silent for a while, thinking of what had happened all those years ago. 'No,' she said finally. 'No, I did not become a nun because I could not marry him whom I loved. I became a nun because I was forced to.'

The prostitute looked at her in surprise. 'Forced to? But that doesn't happen nowadays, does it?'

'Not literally forced,' the nun replied. 'My parents didn't actually drag me off to the nearest convent and shove me into the hands of the Mother Superior. But I realized that things were bad. I had three younger sisters, and my father couldn't afford to provide handsome dowries for each of us. And there was only one son in the family—my elder brother, who seemed to be going nowhere in life. My father tried very hard to get him a job somewhere, but he never wanted to work, so—well, it never worked out. Amma never mentioned it to me, but I could see clearly enough that it was becoming increasingly difficult for Appa to support all of us on the pittance that he earned.'

She stopped, her eyes clouding over with the half-forgotten memories of a youth she had not remembered for many years now.

'Well?' the other woman prompted. 'Couldn't *you* have married the man you loved? Or did he expect a fat dowry too?' There was bitterness in her voice, a cynicism that edged every syllable.

The nun shook her head. 'No, he didn't. At least, I don't think so. But he—he wasn't a Christian, you see. A Brahmin, and from one of those old families that pride themselves on their clans, their lineage. He was terrified of them, of what they would say if he said he wanted to marry a Christian.'

'And you let it go at that?'

The nun stared out of the window, watching the countryside go by. Her gaze was far away, way back in the past. A teenager, looking on at the crumbling of a first love, watching with helpless eyes as the only romance in her life deserted her.

'What could I do?' she replied, in a voice just above a whisper. 'Go and stand at their gate and beg to be taken in? It wasn't as if'—she flushed—'as if he'd done *anything*.' She glanced very briefly at the woman beside her, and was taken aback to see a look of deep sympathy, of understanding. The nun did not need to say more; the prostitute said it for her.

'So you became a nun? Because you couldn't think of anything else to do?'

'Hmm.'

The nun stared down at the coir bag in her lap, looking fixedly down at the crisscross weave of the fibres as she caressed the bag absent-mindedly. The prostitute, in her turn, looked steadily at the nun, her face inscrutable. Then, after about a minute had passed, she said, 'But I was *literally* forced.'

The nun looked up at her.

The kohl-rimmed eyes were hard. 'I never had a mother—she died giving birth to me—and my father disappeared God knows where when I was ten. I think he just got sick of looking after me. An old aunt looked after me for a few years, and then she died. I stayed on in her house, all by myself, trying to make ends meet by doing odd jobs in other people's homes. One day a man came along to my aunt's place, saying he was the landlord and that I had to pay up the rent. I couldn't, of course—so he dragged me off, telling me he'd take me to the police station.'

She paused, and when she continued, her voice was bitter. 'Which he didn't. He took me to a brothel.'

She did not turn to look at the horror in the clear brown eyes of her companion, she did not even pause in the recounting of her sordid tale. 'At first I fought back—it was an awful place—but soon I resigned myself to it. I had, anyway, gone too far to ever come back—nothing could restore to me what I had lost. And I don't just mean my virginity.' The expression on her face hardened perceptibly. 'I lost my childhood, my friends, my dreams, my hopes— everything. *Everything* I cherished and loved was snatched away from me. And I never had any choice.'

There was dead, utter silence. The nun said nothing, just stared on in misery at the prostitute, and the prostitute seemed lost in a world of her own.

Finally, after the bus had traversed a few more kilometres of forest-fringed road, the prostitute turned to the nun. There was a faint smile on her face, and the merest hint of tears in her eyes. 'You must have wondered why I began talking to you,' she said gently. And when the nun looked on quietly, she said, 'Because you reminded me so much of a childhood friend of mine. She and I were the closest of friends—her family were neighbours of ours, while my father was there—and she was about my age. I don't even recall her name now, it's been such a long time. But yes, I do remember her face, and it was like yours. It had the same serenity—and her eyes were like yours, quiet and peaceful. Sounds silly, doesn't it?' she smiled, 'talking of a ten-year old like that. But she was almost angelic. A wonderful person. And when I saw you climb into the bus, the first thought that came to my mind was that wherever she is today, she must be like you.'

The nun still did not say a word.

The bus trundled on, and as it turned a bend, a village appeared in the distance, its red-tiled rooftops visible between the surrounding trees. It was a modest hamlet, much like any of the others on the route but on seeing it, a shadow passed over the nun's face.

She turned to the woman beside her and said quietly, 'This is where I get off.' Her hands were fumbling nervously with the bag, the strap of which she now slung over her shoulder as she prepared to get up.

The prostitute nodded and smiled gently, her features softening momentarily into a somewhat woebegone and innocent beauty. Their eyes met—the whore's dark-rimmed, heavily made-up gaze delving deep into the strangely troubled brown eyes of the nun. Then the prostitute said quietly, 'Thank you.'

She did not say why she thanked the nun. And the nun, in her turn, looked silently at the other woman for a few moments, before beginning to move towards the front of the bus.

The bus halted in a swirl of dust at the village bus stand, a thick pole marked by a battered sign that carried a faded timetable of sorts. A few people standing about waiting for buses gazed curiously at the nun as she stepped off the bus, and then they too looked away, watching the road. The bus waited for just about a minute or so, for any passengers that might be in the mood to get on or get off, and then the driver seemed to lose all patience. He switched gears abruptly, and with a sudden roar of protest, the bus shot off down the road in a cloud of dust, leaving behind the nun, who stood looking at it in a mute, expressionless way.

She remained standing for a while, as if rooted to the spot. Then, slowly and carefully, she made her way to a shack that leaned precariously against the side of a two-storey mansion further down the street. The shack was a frugal-looking structure, consisting of a moth-eaten thatch of palm fronds perched atop four bamboo poles. Below the thatch were a rough wooden table, three equally rough stools, a rusty stove and an old woman with keen eyes that kept a watch on all that happened along the road.

The old woman had been observing the nun as she approached, and when the nun finally came to the shack, she smiled in greeting. 'So you're back,' she said in a hoarse voice, her broken teeth showing in an affectionate grin. 'I have missed you—and I'm sure everybody up at the convent missed you too. Went to meet your mother, didn't you?'

The nun nodded, but did not say anything. After a moment of simply standing there and looking at the old woman, she lowered herself onto one of the stools, pulling it forward towards the table as she did so. Carefully, gently, she put her bag down onto the table and looked up at the old woman, who was regarding her with anxious eyes.

'Is everything all right?' The concern in the voice was apparent.

There was silence for the briefest of moments, and then the nun whispered, 'My mother's dead. She was very ill when I got there, and she just about managed to say goodbye to me.'

There were the usual words of consolation, the shock, the commiseration, the assurance that prayers would be said for the peace of the departed and the solace of the bereaved. The nun sat through it all, and then, in a weary voice, she murmured, 'Could I have a cup of tea, please? I'm very thirsty—and very tired.'

The old woman did not even stop to say yes, she would go and get it straightaway, she simply scurried off, intent on fetching what was so sorely needed.

She was back in the space of a couple of minutes, a slightly battered but clean teacup in hand. The water, obviously, had been boiling in the kettle, ready for whichever customer came by. The nun took the cup, murmured her gratitude, and sipped the tea while the old woman sat down opposite her.

There was a long silence.

After she had half-emptied the cup, the nun spoke of her own accord. She put the cup down, and looked the old woman straight in the eye.

'Mariamma,' she said softly—so softly, in fact, that the old woman had to strain to catch the words—'You have lived so much longer than I have. You know so much more of life than I do.'

Mariamma nodded, her grey head bobbing nervously at this sudden and unprecedented honour bestowed upon her.

'Then,' said the nun, 'tell me if I am wrong to suddenly harbour a grudge against a dead mother—a mother who has left me nothing in life but this—.' She turned out the contents of the bag she had been carrying, and on to the rough table spilled a motley collection of papers, letters, and old photographs. 'This,'—the nun indicated a yellowed photograph of two girls, perhaps about ten years old, knock-kneed and awkward, their faces wreathed in sunny grins, their arms entwined about each other's waists, '—and this, and this—'. A frayed letter, written in a very careful but obviously childish hand, another, in the same handwriting, but now somewhat untidy—and more. More letters, more photographs of the two little girls. Most of all, more letters.

'This is all that my mother left me,' said the nun, in a flat voice from which even the bitterness had been completely drained. 'This, and the confession that she had deliberately blocked every letter, every note, every attempt that my best friend had made, to tell me why she had suddenly disappeared from my life. My mother simply told me that she knew what had happened to my friend—and that she wanted to shield me from such filth. And that was why she never told me.'

She looked down sadly at the heap of memories lying on the table, neglected and forgotten and full of the desperation of a frightened girl trying to make contact with one whom she loved. A girl who had grown up and was now no more than a stranger on a bus by now far away.

'Tell me, Mariamma,' said the nun, 'am I so very evil to resent what my mother did?'

But all Mariamma could do was sit and stare at her with scared, unhappy eyes.

Collector of Junk

AMMA IS PART of my earliest memory. A thin, strong woman, her greying hair caught in an untidy bun. Even when I was small, Amma had white in her hair and fine wrinkles around her eyes. Wrinkles that deepened as she grew older, hands that grew more leather-like. When I think of her, I am reminded of her faintly nasal voice, the bright eyes that never missed a thing.

Yes, Amma is part of my earliest memories.

Of anything. Of everything.

I remember her making me sit on a small plastic stool. A blue stool, the blue of a noon sky, with streaks of dried soap scum on its flat surfaces. I scraped at one with the edge of a fingernail, and Amma batted my hand away. 'Don't do that, Munni.' She placed a doll in my lap. A battered, grubby doll, discarded by some rich kid. Most of its golden hair had come out. What remained was dirty and limp. 'Play with that.'

And, later, when I was old enough, I remember Amma handing me a large paraat, an aluminium platter with high sloping sides, a huge heap of raw rice in its centre. Rice, with the odd pebble here, the little clod of dried mud there. The occasional chaff.

By time time, Amma did not need to tell me what to

do with the rice. I was eight years old, responsible enough
to know I had to carefully pick out every little thing that
shouldn't have been there. That shouldn't end up in one of
the plates Amma served to the men who ate at her tiny food
stall outside the flour mill.

I would sift through the rice, throwing out all the
unwanted bits, the rubbish. Amma would be nearby,
chopping vegetables or stirring the dal simmering on the
primitive kerosene stove. And there would invariably be
someone beside her, talking. Kallu, for instance.

Kallu was a hanger-on outside the flour mill. He couldn't
have been old—perhaps in his mid-thirties—but he had a
shock of grey hair and wore a perpetually harassed look
that made him appear much older. I didn't ever see Kallu
go inside the mill, but now and then, someone—usually the
watchman at the gate—would summon him. There would
be a muted conversation, and Kallu would go off down the
street on an errand.

'It's a hard life, Amma,' he would say. She was not his
mother, but he still called her Amma. I resented it. 'They
will not give me a job, even though I have pleaded and
promised. It was a mistake, Amma. I knew it even then. I
would turn back time if I could. But they will not forgive
me.' Amma would go on with her work, and I—glancing
sideways, trying not to let them notice me eavesdropping—
would wonder if her tears were because of the onions she
was chopping or because she felt sorry for Kallu.

'Everybody should be allowed a second chance, Amma,'
Kallu would say, and Amma would nod. 'Yes,' she would
say. Or *no*, whatever it took to let Kallu know she was
listening. 'And look, they do call me every now and then
to do something for them. If they can trust me to do that,

why not give me a job, hanh?' Amma would nod, and if her hands were not greasy or stained with turmeric or wet with tomato juice, she would pat him on the knee of his shapeless, frayed trousers. I would gloat silently. Not for Kallu were Amma's warm hugs, her brusquely affectionate way of wiping away tears, or her kisses when I hurt myself. Those were all mine, and I guarded them jealously. Kallu had to be content with a brief pat on the knee now and then.

'Why does he come and complain to you, Amma?' I asked once, when I was about twelve—old enough to have an opinion on what went on around me. Old enough, even, to consider my opinion worth airing.

'He's not complaining. Just talking.' Amma was grinding ginger and garlic, and the smell rose strong and sharp from the massive grinding-stone.

'But he's telling you all the time about how bad things are for him. What's wrong? What happened to Kallu? Why is he so'—I groped for a word, my vocabulary and experience not yet able to find expressions for things so elusive—'so strange?'

'Kallu is not strange,' Amma said. 'He just has his problems. All of us do.'

Amma and I certainly had our problems. The little two-yards-by-two tin shed we called home baked in the summer, clattered and leaked in the monsoon, and did little to keep out the cold in the winter. All our clothes were hand-me-downs. Our food was invariably the last bits of whatever had been left over from Amma's lunchtime sales of dal and rice, vegetables and rotis.

Yes, we had our troubles, but Amma never spoke of them. Whom would she speak to? I was too young to

understand, and we had no relatives. Our neighbours—
their roofs covered with tarpaulins weighed down with
bricks, their children running snotty-nosed and naked in
the lane behind, the men sprawling and drinking cheap
country liquor in the evening—they had more troubles than
we did. Or so Amma said. And so, too, I could hear and
see for myself.

'He beats me, Amma,' Kusum would say, when she came
by now and then, lowering herself onto the charpai. She
must have been pretty once, but six years of wedded life and
four children had wrung all semblance of beauty away. The
bruises on her face, the scars on her arm—her husband's
favourite means of chastizing his wife was to press the end
of a smouldering beedi on her arm—all were proof of what
Kusum went through.

She would sit opposite Amma, hugging herself and
talking about her husband, her children, the pain, the
suffering. Never once did she offer to help Amma, even
though Amma would be working. Working all the time,
washing clothes, sweeping, mending a torn garment. No,
Kusum would not help. Kusum would sit and moan.

As would all the others. They each had their own miseries.
Some were like Kusum, battered and marked with wounds
that shouted out their tales of woe. Others bore sorrows
less visible. Shambhu, for instance, who used to come every
Sunday, when the mill was closed and Amma wheeled the
food stall and set it up closer to home. Shambhu used to
sell vegetables. Limp spinach and yellowing cucumbers,
onions streaked with black and tomatoes that were either
too green or too pulpy. 'I cannot afford good vegetables,'
he would say to Amma as he spread out his wares on the
ragged tarpaulin next to Amma's stall. 'You know how it is,
Amma. You know what I've been through.'

'What has he been through, Amma?' I whispered one day, when Shambhu had gone off to his square of tarpaulin to attend to one of his rare customers, a woman who looked as if she couldn't even afford what Shambhu had to sell.

'None of your business, Munni.'

'But you know, don't you? Why don't you tell me? Maybe we can do something to help.'

She shook her head. 'He isn't looking for help. Just someone to listen.'

I thought them all pitiable, but also contemptible. People with no backbone. Kallu could have moved on from the mill. Kusum, if only she put her mind to it, could stand up to her husband. Shambhu, whatever he'd been through, could put it behind him and get a move on. Why did they all have to come and waste Amma's time?

If it had been only them, I might have been more forgiving, less possessive of Amma's time. But these were only three people, three of many. Some came by once in a blue moon, stopping on the way to somewhere else, long enough to tell Amma of their many sorrows. Some were more regular. Some were strangers, people cropping up out of the blue.

There was the woman who was sitting beside the hand pump one day when Amma and I went to fill water. She was a fat woman, her face sloping outward from a narrow forehead to a many-chinned jaw that sat almost neckless on her shoulders. She waddled when she moved, one plump hand resting on her knee as she made her way forward. Amma offered to help her draw water—the woman had brought along a red plastic bucket—and that was all the excuse the woman needed.

Amma shooed me off with a whispered 'Go and play if

you want to, Munni. I will be back in a while.' As I walked away, I could see the woman easing herself down onto the wooden bench nearby. She was already beginning to chat with Amma, introducing herself, asking Amma how old I was, where Amma's husband was.

I did not go off to play—the children in the huts around ours were too small for me, their games too childish. I went into our little shed, instead, and found work for myself. There was always work. Cowdung cakes to be made—smelly work, this, mixing the dung with chaff, and moulding it into cowpats, to be dried in the sun and used as fuel. A fire to be lit. The floor to be swept and mopped.

I had finished all of that and was thinking of returning to the hand pump to see if Amma was all right when she came in.

She stumbled in, rather. Looking gaunt and exhausted, her eyes sunken. As I rushed towards her, asking what was wrong, had she run into trouble—she waved a hand at me, weakly. 'No, Munni. Nothing, it's nothing so terrible. I just need to sit quietly for a while. Get me a glass of water.'

I had never seen Amma in such a state. I brought the water, and the little bamboo hand fan. 'No, it's all right,' she mumbled. 'I'm not ill, Munni. Just leave me alone for half an hour, child. An hour,' she amended.

So I went out. I sat on the edge of the pavement bordering the slum, and watched the neighbourhood boys playing with a half-deflated football, kicking it about. I listened in on conversations. I heard someone turn on a radio from which Hindi film songs blared.

I heard nothing. I saw nothing. I was there in body, but my spirit was back there, in that tiny room, hovering around Amma. What had happened to her?

Finally, when I could not bear it any more, I returned to the room but stayed outside. I had shut the door behind me when I had left, in an attempt to deter passersby who might be inclined to come in and pester Amma. But the window was open, and if I peered in at an angle, I could see Amma sitting cross-legged on the thin mattress. In her lap was an old cardboard shoebox, discoloured and frayed at the corners. I had seen it once, in the bottom of the trunk in which Amma kept all the odds and ends we dared not leave unattended while we were out: our clothes, blankets, quilt, extra pots and pans. I had seen this shoebox there, and never wondered what it contained.

Amma hunched over it now. I saw her shoulders shake. I heard the sobs, low and soft. For the first time in my life, I saw Amma break down. Amma, always strong, suddenly looked like one of the many poor, complaining, sad souls who used to wash up at our door. It frightened me.

The next minute, I got a glimpse of something glittering as it caught the light. Amma had straightened slightly, lifting something from the box. She held it up, as if taking a closer look at it, and I saw that it was a necklace. A cheap, common little necklace, of the sort I used to wear when I was small. Blue glass beads strung on a red thread. Amma looked at it for an instant, then hugged it to her thin chest and cried.

I slunk away. I could not bear to see any more. It was embarrassing to watch Amma fall apart. I hurried out, going into the lane that separated our homes from the smarter houses beyond the park. I made my way into the park, and sat there for a while, shaking. When darkness began to fall, I finally got up and headed home, dreading all the way what I'd find when I got there. Would Amma still be crying, no longer the Amma I had known all these years?

But no. She was back to normal, or almost. She still looked weary, and her face was puffy. But she took me to task swiftly enough for having stayed out so long after sunset. And even though she didn't say much the rest of the evening, I could tell that her silence was not because she was angry with me, but because she was disturbed.

Everything was too awkward, too raw. I stayed quiet through the rest of the evening. It was only the next day, when we were scouring the pots and pans after lunch, that I spoke up. 'Amma,' I said, 'What happened yesterday? Why were you so upset?'

Amma's hands slowed, but she did not stop her work. 'Munni, you are too meddlesome for your own good,' she said.

I was not to be put off so easily. 'Tell me, Amma. What happened? Why were you crying over that necklace? Those beads—did that fat woman give them to you?'

Her head jerked up at that. 'Don't call her *that fat woman*. Her name is Sughra. And she didn't give me the necklace.'

'All right, Sughra, then. But did *she* say something? You were with her when I left,' I said accusingly. 'She must have said something to upset you.'

Amma sighed. 'She was not to blame. She did not know that what she said would sadden me—that was not her intention.'

'Then what was her intention? And you didn't know this woman—this Sughra—before, isn't that so? A total stranger?' I saw Amma's grudging nod, and ploughed on, even more indignant now than I had been a moment earlier. 'And you let a stranger do this to you, Amma! *Why*?'

Amma plunged the plastic mug into the bucket of water beside her and rinsed the paraat. I thought she had decided to end the conversation there. But when I had scrubbed the tawa, cleaning it of every last particle of blackened flour, I heard Amma say, 'Do you know, Munni, what is the worst thing that can happen to a human being?'

I frowned. She was not looking at me; she was focused on the pot she held. 'Death?'

Amma laughed. 'You are a child, even if you don't consider yourself one any longer. Death is not a bad thing, except for those who are left behind to miss those who are gone. Death is—*relief*. When you die, you are left with no worries. No wondering where your next meal is coming from, no wondering whether you will be strong enough to go out to work when you wake up. No fears. No nothing.'

'You talk as if you've experienced death,' I said, jeeringly.

'I may have,' Amma admitted with a small smile that made me shiver. 'Anybody who's lived as many years as I have has seen death. I have seen many die, Munni.' She began scrubbing, her shoulders moving rhythmically under her faded choli. 'But that was not what I was saying. Death is not the worst thing that can happen. The worst thing that can happen is to be left without anybody by your side.'

'What do you mean?' I asked. 'There's always somebody around.' I groped for an example, something to support my statement. 'Even if you are not there—like it happened last evening—there is always someone else. There are the neighbours.'

'You can be lonely even surrounded by people.'

I thought Amma was being insufferably vague. Pretentious and philosophical. I frowned, willing to let the topic die a natural death. Amma did not seem inclined to pursue it further either, she went on with her work, and shortly after, with Kallu arriving, we forgot all about it.

And we went back to life. With Kallu and Kusum and Shambhu, and all the others—even Sughra, the fat woman whom I resented for having made Amma such a wreck that day—continuing to haunt our home. Continuing to take up Amma's time. Continuing to blabber on, fill her ears with all their unending woes.

Then one day, when I was about eighteen, Amma died.

Yes. Just like that. Out of the blue.

I woke up in the morning to find that Amma—who was usually up before me—was still asleep. I supposed she hadn't been able to sleep well the previous night. It was like that sometimes; Amma would toss and turn, and go out every half hour to the shared and very smelly latrine at the end of the lane. Then, the next morning, her eyes would be red and her face bloated when she woke. I had my instructions—if I was up and she was still asleep, I had to wake her up by the time our neighbour turned on his radio to listen to the news.

So I waited, and when I heard the distinctive tune that heralded the start of the news, I went and shook Amma's shoulder. 'Wake up, Amma.'

But she never did.

The neighbour was the person I first ran to when I realized what had happened. Within minutes, everybody had clustered around. Some curious, some solicitous, some helpful. One old man I remembered as being one of Amma's frequent visitors took over the task of organizing the ragtag crowd, sending someone off to the cremation ground, telling some of the women to attend to the body. Taking me to his own home, where I could sit with his daughter-in-law.

It was later that day that Sughra turned up. I don't know why she came. Perhaps she had heard the buzz of gossip—the more gory or shocking the news, the faster it spreads in our neighbourhood, and Amma's sudden demise was certainly shocking. Perhaps Sughra hadn't heard, and had merely happened to come by to chat with Amma, like she did so often. Whatever it was, when she discovered what had happened, she came looking for me. A flabby figure swathed in a pink salwar-kurta. A purple dupatta flung untidily over her head and shoulders. Dithering on the threshold, before finally stepping in.

I recall little of what happened. I remember Sughra holding my hand, leading me home. I remember looking down at Amma, now lying flat on her back, covered with a white sheet up to her neck. Somebody had draped a garland of orange marigolds around her neck, their scent battling that of the burning incense sticks stuck into a crack in the wood of the charpai.

I remember seeing the men pick up the charpai and leave, a small procession of sombre faces, some of them clad in white, the majority in their everyday clothes.

The rest, I do not remember. I do not remember when Sughra took me to her home. I have only faint recollections of how it was at her home, with her thin, grey-haired husband and her many children, from the scruffy-haired toddler with the runny nose to the skinny young man who looked so like his father.

One day, I came to. Almost as if somebody had wiped the windowpane of my mind, sweeping away the dust. I hurt, I throbbed. Sughra saw it, and sitting down next to me, said, 'I understand your pain. Believe me, Munni. I do.' She folded her hands in her lap and looked at them, at the dirty nails and the fat, work-roughened palms. 'My youngest daughter died not too long ago, you know.'

No, I did not know. I wished she would leave me alone.

'That first day when I met your Amma—I was grieving for my girl. My Roshni, such a sweet child she was… really roshni, the light of our lives. She was outside, playing in the street. Just seven years old. Too young to die. But can one stop destiny?' She shook her head, her jowls wobbling against her fat neck. I felt sick. Sorry, too. But I did not want to hear how Roshni had died.

And Sughra did not tell me how Roshni had died.

'They brought her in,' she said. 'She looked as if she was asleep. Just a little dusty, that's all. And the necklace she loved so much had broken. It had blue beads, you know, and the string snapped. There were blue beads in the lane outside, and in the gutter. Someone's toddler was picking them up, one bead at a time, when I went outside.'

'Did—did you tell Amma that?' I asked in a hoarse whisper. And when Sughra nodded yes, I sat back, trying to reason it out. Sughra asked me what the matter was, but I shook my head. Later, in the solitude of the corner of the room I had been allotted, when neither Sughra nor her brood were around, I unrolled the bundle of belongings I had brought with me. Amma's shoebox was there, and when I opened it, there, too, was the necklace. I took it in my hands, running the smooth, glossy beads through my fingers, wondering.

Finally, I took it to Sughra. She blinked when she saw it.

'Was this it?' I asked. I couldn't think how it could be, but I couldn't see any other connection between Roshni's death, and that long-ago day when Amma had hunched over these beads and wept, after meeting Sughra for the first time. Had Amma happened to come along when that child was gathering up the beads, while Sughra mourned her daughter? Had Amma picked up some of those beads and gone away, stringing them onto a thread of her own? Stashing them away?

It made no sense.

'No,' Sughra said. 'It isn't. These are the blue of—of a kingfisher's wing. And they're large, much larger than Roshni's beads. Those were small. Small beads for a small girl. And they were pale blue, like a sky in spring. And with tiny golden specks here and there...' She had taken the necklace from me when I had offered it, and she now held it up between the fingers of both hands, framing her fat, tear-streaked face in that oval of bright, glittering blue.

'This belonged to your Amma,' she said. 'She told me about it, many days ago. Some time after Roshni died, the day I first met your Amma.' She lowered the necklace, caught it up in one hand, and held it out to me. 'I told your Amma about Roshni, and about Roshni's blue beads. Then she told me about these beads. They were her daughter's, before she died.'

Amma had never told me about a daughter. *I had had a sister*? I stared at Sughra, a thousand questions whirling through my mind. I did not know which to express first. Which of the questions, or even which of the emotions. The bafflement, the hurt, the betrayal—that Amma had never told me. And the very next moment, contrition for that thought. Amma must have mourned my sister all these years. Carried that pain within her, sheltering me from it.

'No,' Sughra said, as if I had, indeed, spoken. 'No, she was not your sister. 'Your Amma—she was not your real mother, you know. She only ever gave birth once, and that was to the girl who died. She died, like my Roshni did, even before she became a woman. Both she and her father died of cholera. And you—your Amma found you, a baby, wailing in a ruined hut. Your parents had died in the epidemic.' She let the string of beads run through her fingers. 'She brought you home.'

It stuck in my chest, in my throat. I felt as if someone had wiped out all my past and replaced it with someone else's past, someone else's life.

'She never told me,' I said.

'She did not tell anyone anything,' Sughra said. I looked up at her and asked her how *she* knew, and she said, 'Your Amma told me, that day. I showed her my Roshni's beads, and it made your Amma cry. I did not know why, then, so she told me. We had a long chat that day. As if we had not just met, but had been the best of friends for years.'

Yes. I remembered waiting for Amma that evening.

'She told me, when she was leaving that day, that she had never told anybody the things she had said to me. She told me not to tell anyone, either. But I think she would want you to know, Munni. Perhaps she meant to tell you, when you were a woman. She is gone, and who knows, perhaps someday suddenly I too will be gone, and then who will tell you?'

I did not say anything. I could not think of anything to say.

'Your Amma,' said Sughra, caressing the beads like a rosary, 'was a kabaadi, a collector of junk. You know what kabaadis do, don't you? They gather junk. Pay for it. Take it home. Sort through it. Sell it.'

This, I thought, with a stab of irritation, was nonsense. Sughra's mind was wandering. Amma had not been a

kabaadi, Amma had run a food stall. I knew the ins and
outs of Amma's life. She had never collected junk.

'No, not literally,' Sughra said, even before I could
interrupt. 'She paid for it, though. In tears.' She glanced
up at me, the necklace forgotten for the time being—I
wondered now if Sughra had even been thinking of the
necklace, all this time she'd been fiddling with it. 'And of
course she didn't sell anything. What she collected was the
refuse of other people's lives. Their sorrows, their shame.
Our sorrows,' she said, correcting herself. '*Our* shame.'

I stared back.

'You think I'm mad, don't you, Munni?' Sughra said.
'I suppose I am. Your Amma would have understood.
Perhaps you will, too, one day. Years from now.' She took
my hand, patted it, the string of beads cool and hard against
my knuckles, Sughra's hands rough and plump in contrast.
'Your Amma listened. She listened to anybody who had
burdens to share. She listened whenever someone needed a
shoulder to cry on. All of us have pains, Munni. Body pains
and heart pains and mind pains and money pains. Secrets
that can smother our spirits. Sorrows too deep-seated to
be wept over any more, but which eat away at us from the
inside. Do you—do you understand what I'm saying?'

I nodded. Yes, I think I did understand. I remembered
Kallu. And Kusum, with her bruises and burns. I remembered
Shambhu. I remembered Sughra. I remembered the countless
others who had come to Amma, drawn like moths to a
flame.

'She never turned anyone away,' I mumbled.

'And she never told anybody her own worries,' Sughra
added. 'Yes, she was like that. A kabaadi, gathering all the
debris of the world and taking it into herself.' She let go of

my hand and stood up, wincing as she did so. 'She was a good woman, your Amma. I miss her.'

So do I, I thought of saying.

'Are you coming in?' Sughra asked. 'I'll make tea.'

Good masala chai, brewed till it was thick and sweet and aromatic with ginger and cardamom. We sat with our hands curled around the steel glasses, breathing in the fragrance of the tea. Hoarding the precious glory of it, drinking it one tiny sip at a time. Finally, I looked up at Sughra and said, 'Tell me about Roshni.'

And she did. About how lovable Roshni had been, about everything that made her sweet. The way she lisped, the unintentionally hilarious things she did. Her dimples, her curls. Her death.

Sughra talked on, on and on, until the tea was over and darkness was falling.

Then, with a smile—a genuine smile, welling up from the depths of her, transforming her face into one of beauty—she stroked my cheek, as if I were Roshni, the daughter she had lost. 'You are your mother's child,' she said softly.

And both of us knew that she was not talking about the woman who had given birth to me.

The Letter

IT HAD BEEN many, many days since the postman had brought anything other than the monthly money order, so it came as a bit of a shock for Inimai to hear him say, 'There's a letter for you today.'

He shoved the yellowed envelope into her trembling hand and pedalled off, leaving her staring at the letter. She gazed wistfully at the postman cycling away. There had been a time, long, long ago when postmen were like family. They would stop at each house to exchange gossip, to read out letters to those who could not read, to be company to the lonely. But postmen now, like everybody else, were busy. Inimai sighed, and clutching the letter, shuffled painfully and slowly to Radha's house. Radha, with her gleaming tresses and kindly eyes, Radha, beauteous, bountiful—Radha, who would never refuse Inimai.

'It's from Shankar, Amma,' Radha said, her voice as excited as if the letter was from her son, not Inimai's. 'Let's see what he says—he's coming, Amma! Wait—I'll read out what he's written.'

Five minutes later, Inimai was on her way home, her heart buoyant, her limp pronounced as she hurried home to cook, clean and wait in eager anticipation. How long was it since they had come? Three years? No, surely less. Hadn't

Shankar brought them all home when his baby daughter was born? That must have been a year and a half ago. Inimai did not remember.

But who cared how long it was, what mattered was that they were coming. She smiled a bright, toothless smile to herself as she thought of her grandchildren running in the coconut grove, splashing along the stream, sitting in enraptured silence, listening to her stories. There would be laughter and talking, not the pitiful silence which Inimai tried unsuccessfully to disperse by humming to herself.

So much had to be done. She had swept the house that morning, but she would sweep it again. And wash the red oxide courtyard, do the dusting, fill the little brass vase with jasmine flowers. And do the cooking. As she bustled about, she wondered what to make. Murukkus, of course: those crisp fried spirals which the children loved, and dosai, sambhar, coconut chutney, payasam—payasam was Shankar's favourite. She smiled as she remembered how he'd gulp down huge bowlfuls of it. 'Nobody makes payasam the way you do, Amma.'

It took a long time, but by sunset, everything was done. The beds made, the floor washed. The rice ground, the batter made for the dosais. The payasam, fragrant and sugary, was cooling on the veranda, the sambhar was simmering on the earthen stove. Inimai had ground fresh chutney and pounded the mulaga podi till its rich spiciness permeated the kitchen.

They should be here by now.

Perhaps their train was late. These city trains often were.

At seven o'clock, Inimai hobbled to the railway station. It would give her more time with them when they came.

She sat on a wooden bench on the platform. A lone figure, watching, waiting.

Eight o'clock. No train.

Nine.

Ten.

The train came, and Inimai, in the dim yellow light of the platform lantern, watched people get off the train.

No Shankar. No daughter-in-law, no children.

'No more trains tonight, Amma,' the stationmaster said gently. 'Shall I get the guard to take you home?'

But Inimai shook her head sadly and limped home alone, a quiet, disappointed figure.

Many miles away, Shankar slept peacefully, unaware that a long-ago letter, promising a trip that had never materialized, had been retrieved from a forgotten pigeonhole by an underworked postal clerk and delivered to his mother. Unaware that Radha, in her excitement, had not noticed that the letter was two years too late. Unaware that his mother, alone in her house, wept as she put away the payasam and scattered the wilted jasmine outside her window.

Two Doors

THE BALCONY DOOR is a double one. Not two leaves fitting neatly together in a marriage of wood and steel, but one door opening in, the other opening out. The inner door is a wooden one with a glass panel, the outer an iron grille. To keep the monkeys out.

They are not permanent residents here, the monkeys. Passersby, rather, coming when the mangoes begin to ripen on the tree outside. Opportunists, Kamini thinks as she stares out at them. This troop arrived early this morning; she could hear them in the branches even as she brushed her teeth. The house, with Vishal gone to Bangalore for his conference, is silent. There is a comfort in the silence. She need not cook breakfast, toast will do just fine. She need not make lunch, or dinner. She can order pizza, or make herself a sandwich. Maggi noodles, whatever.

Even before the thought is over, another automatically takes its place. You have to eat healthy, you must get your vitamins. And don't forget your supplements, the ubiquinol and inositol and the dozen other bottles lined neatly up on the shelf. Remember to do your pranayama. The yoga, too, sitting with your legs folded and your knees jutting out on either side so that your vagina gapes. It strengthens the womb, it will help when it is time for the baby to come.

What baby, she thinks. *What baby?* The baby that has been missing these ten years of her marriage?

'Come on now, when are you giving us some good news?' Her sister-in-law had teased when Kamini and Vishal had returned from their honeymoon in Manali. Just a week's holiday, since Vishal, less than a month into a new job, couldn't afford to take more leave.

'Kamini's hopeful of a 25 per cent increment this year,' Vishal had said, and had burst out laughing at the bewilderment on his sister's face. 'You wanted good news, nutjob. You've got it. Happy?'

'You know what I mean,' Vidushi had pouted. 'Hey, bhabhi. Hey?' Nudge, wink.

Nudge, wink. Nudge. Wink, wink, wink. From the younger lot, Vishal's cousins, his two sisters, even a distant niece who was in her precocious teens. 'I want to be an aunty. Come on, bhabhi!' That incessant and unselfconscious egging on to produce a baby. To have more sex, Kamini used to think. In a society as prudish as Delhi even in 2005, to be urging people on to get into bed and start making babies. Just because they had got married, and a marriage meant you had to start procreating at once?

The older lot had been sedately patient, Vishal's mother and his aunts smiling in a smug way whenever they had met the couple. There had even been, to Kamini's embarrassed relief, admonitions. 'Leave them be, Vidushi,' Ma had said. 'What will happen, will happen.'

Ma had known, of course, that it would take time. A month, at least, if they kept at it all through her fertile period. Perhaps, if the gods were not too kind, a month or two more. And, if Kamini were as shy and demure as a good bride was supposed to be, she would not tell anyone until

she was absolutely sure, and had been to a gynaecologist…
four months? Five?

**

Kamini goes to the kitchen to have her flax seeds, her glass
of water. The five almonds. The piece of fruit. As she's eating
the mango, she makes a note of today's basal temperature.
97.2 degrees. After these four years, she can make sense of
her cycle without even trying to. Her ovulation is at least
four days away. Vishal will be back home by then. He can
spend the day at home, in bed with her, the day he returns:
it's a Sunday. Monday will be a problem, because he has to
go to work. Sex will be possible only when he comes home
at night, and she thinks the ovum might have ruptured by
then. There must be sperm in her when the ovum ruptures,
if there is to be a chance at fertilization.

Kamini is not supposed to have toast for breakfast: oats
with vegetables is what the nutritionist has recommended.
But she cannot be bothered with that today, not with Vishal
away. She wants this day for herself. To eat what she wants.
To sit and read, to gaze out of the window at the world
going by.

'How can you sit around and daydream all day long?'
Vishal had asked her, the second day of their honeymoon.
They had known each other three months then, and had
met all of four times before they had got married. No
wonder they were only getting to know each other now.

'Don't tell me you sit in your office and stare out of the
window,' Vishal had said as he pulled on his T-shirt.

'Only when my work for the day is done,' had been her
rejoinder. 'And that never happens.' Which he knew well

enough, because on the one evening when he had landed up unannounced at home, it had been to find Mummy and Papa alone. Kamini never got home before eight, and that only if she were lucky. Even luckier if she did not bring home work.

'You're very keen on a career, aren't you?'

'Why shouldn't I be?' She had bristled. 'My parents put a lot into my education. I put a lot into it, too. If all of that is just so that I can sit at home and look decorative—'

'For God's sake! I wasn't being critical. Good for you, and good for me.' He had hugged her around the shoulders, in an embrace more comradely than romantic. 'I don't want a wife who stews at home all day long and then whines about being bored. You won't do that, will you?'

She didn't. She didn't have the time to do it. Or the temperament.

**

The phone rings. It is Ma, Vishal's mother. 'You did not phone,' she says accusingly. Peevishly. By now she should know that Kamini is not the kind to dutifully phone every morning just to ask how everybody is, whether they slept well, and what they are planning to do today. Ma knows it, and the realization that her wishes do not matter to Kamini irks her.

But it was she, this woman with the hennaed hair, with her proven fertility and her four children, who had been the first to whom Kamini had listened when it came to the matter of babies.

'You aren't pregnant, are you?' Ma had asked, that long-ago day in mid-winter, as they sat on the lawn, eating walnuts and jaggery while they waited for the masala chai to cool a bit. 'Vishal hasn't said anything.'

Six months had passed since their wedding. Six months, to the day. The question had been well-timed.

Kamini had shaken her head and murmured a no.

There had followed a long silence. Accusation, unspoken but loud, had hung in the air. The tea had gone cold, its surface covered over with a skin, when Ma had spoken again. 'Don't delay it too much,' she had said, her voice carefully neutral. 'I know your work is important, but this is, too.'

Kamini had not voiced her indignation, not to her mother-in-law and not to her husband. Years of careful upbringing had taught her that you did not argue with your elders. You could argue with the establishment, you could question the government, you could stand up for your rights—but anybody a generation older, and known to you, was to be respected. They were untouchable, unquestionable. Not always correct, no human being could be. But you did not talk back.

And Vishal? It was pointless. She had still not been sure how he would react to criticism of his mother's criticism, but she had not wanted to rock the boat. More than that, she had come to realize that Vishal, at any rate, was in no hurry to have children. Or even, really, to make love to her. The heady euphoria, the passion and steam of the honeymoon, had been just that: restricted to the honeymoon. When they left Manali, they left all of that behind them too.

That winter day, sitting with numb hands wrapped around a cold teacup, she had thought back and tried to remember when they had last made love. It had been on their honeymoon.

'When is he coming back?' Ma asks now, her voice tired, irritated.

'Sunday. First flight in the morning. He should be home by eleven or so.'

'Hmm. Then I don't suppose the two of you will come over for lunch?'

'I don't know, Ma,' Kamini says. She leaves it at that. She is sick of the disapproval, the suspicion, the anger that is now no longer suppressed. On either side. She is still civil, and Ma is, too. On Diwali and Karva Chauth and other festivals, when they meet, they even exchange hugs and put up a show of mutual affection. But both of them know that this is a farce, no more.

'All right,' Ma says. And, just like that, she hangs up. No goodbye, no take care of yourself. Nothing.

* * *

Kamini does not remember when it was that she began to think that they should have a baby. Perhaps it was at a family wedding, when two other cousins—both younger than her—showed up, proudly displaying their pregnancies. Perhaps it was Fauzia, her boss, going on maternity leave. Perhaps it was the slow realization that she had been married four years now and there had been no babies. Or perhaps she had been told so often by friends and relatives, some of them curious, some snide, some openly and unashamedly interfering, that no woman was complete without being a mother, that it had got to her.

How blatant and unafraid people were, she had thought, whenever she read a book or watched a movie in which someone jumped into bed with another someone whom they barely knew without a second thought. She had been too shy to even suggest sex to Vishal. Too shy, too tired. As the years had gone by, work had not eased, on the contrary, it had grown. They had settled, too, into the placid and predictable routine of a couple married much longer than they had been. Secure, comfortable. Not in love, she knew that much: they may have been briefly infatuated with each other in the early months of the marriage, but that fizz had gone. Their idea of quality time together, as Vishal put it, was to watch a movie and eat out. After which they would come home, he to flop down in front of the TV, she to have a bath and get into bed with a book. To doze off still reading, and get up to the alarm.

'How about a baby?' she had blurted out one day. It was a Saturday morning, and Vishal had been reading the newspaper when she emerged from the bathroom.

'Huh? What baby? Who's having a baby?'

'We should,' she had said, not looking at him.

'Why?'

Because all your relatives want us to, she thought of saying. Because my friends and colleagues are having babies and I stick out like a sore thumb. Because I'm nearly thirty, and if I don't have a baby soon—and she had stopped there, cutting off that thought. None of those reasons fitted. None of them were valid. And she could not say that she truly wanted a baby, that she yearned for a child. That was not the reality. She did not feel maternal. Not in the least.

'We can't afford a baby,' Vishal had said, turning a page. 'Do you know how much children cost these days? The education, the medical expenses, all the trappings? We can't afford it. Not now.'

She had wanted to say then that everybody around them

seemed to be able to afford it well enough—even their maid, who had three children of her own—but Kamini had said nothing. It had not mattered so much.

Two weeks later, Vishal's younger brother had died. He had been twenty-seven, seemingly healthy. But he had collapsed at a party one evening, and by the time his friends had got him to a hospital, he was dead. Cardiac arrest, said the doctors.

Kamini did not know whether that made Vishal realize, on his own, that life could not be depended upon, or whether his mother had a say in it. Did Ma tell Vishal that he had to have children, he had to make sure the family name was carried forward into another generation? Vidushi and the younger sister didn't matter, they would get married and become part of other families. This family, Vishal's, hers, now depended on them having children. Ma was quite capable of being blunt.

So, in a matter of days, they went from near-abstinence to near-orgies. If something that lacked either love or lust could be called an orgy. When it was driven by nothing more than desperation, when pleasure had no part in it.

Six months were to pass before she—it was she, now plucking up the courage to say it out aloud—said, 'It's not working. Perhaps there's something wrong? Perhaps we should go to a doctor?'

* * *

She goes out onto the smaller balcony, the one enclosed by mesh, where spider plants hang from hooks on poles and two whopping big monsteras, each leaf larger than a dinner plate and with the most perfectly etched holes in it, flank the doorway. It is cool here, cool and quiet. On the other side of the flat, with the monkey-infested balcony seeming part of a different house, a different city. Delhi can be so contrary, she thinks, as she plucks a couple of fragile white flowers off a spider plant and draws the long cream-and-green striped leaves close to her face. She takes a deep breath. The plant smells of nothing. But ever since someone told her that spider plants are good as air purifiers, because they convert carbon monoxide into oxygen, she has convinced herself that sniffing the leaves must be good for her.

She chuckles to herself. It is a mirthless sound. Sniffing leaves? She has never sniffed anything. Not glue, not anything vaguely not-done, as her mother would say. Kamini has been a *good* girl. A good woman, good in the boringly predictable way of staid middle-class Indian housewives. Not the ones you read about in the newspapers, the ones who run away with the neighbourhood milkman or have affairs with their brothers-in-law. No, she has been the paragon of virtue. Again, one of her mother's favourite idioms. Paragon of virtue. Quiet, obedient, no-drinking, no-smoking, no-swearing. No child-bearing, either, and that has negated all her virtues. In Ma's eyes, Kamini is nothing because she has not borne a child.

It had taken six months more for Vishal to agree to go to a doctor. One of those fertility clinics. Tests, more tests. 'You're both clear,' the gynaecologist had said. 'Have you been trying, eh? Naturally?'

'We have been,' Kamini had mumbled. Vishal, sitting stiffly upright beside her, had said nothing unless it was addressed specifically to him. He was mortified, she knew. Embarrassed that he had not been able to manage something as basic as fathering a child. Not that fathering would end at impregnating her, of course. But that would come later.

'Then we should go in for an IU,' the gynae had said, scribbling on the sheet of paper before her.

They had. And when that had not worked, an IVF. 'It doesn't matter,' the doctor had said comfortingly. There was something very matter-of-fact in the way she spoke, something that had suggested that this failure was nothing to be distressed about. That she hadn't really expected results from the IU. That the IVF would magically implant a baby in Kamini's womb.

Kamini still remembers that first procedure, her feet feeling like blocks of ice as she lay on the operating table, legs spread wide apart. Hearing someone—an irritated voice, one of a team that had descended on her—saying, 'This patient isn't co-operating. She doesn't relax.' And someone else, a man, quiet-voiced and gentle-eyed, who was looking into a monitor, telling her, 'Pray. That helps distract you.'

Yes, good advice. Pray. She had prayed. Prayed then and over the next eighteen days, trying to wish a child into existence. Stepping carefully through life, sleeping long hours, breathing deep, thinking good thoughts. There had been the quiet confidence that nine months from now, she would be holding her baby in her arms. She had begun planning, surfing the net for advice on parenting, window-shopping for baby clothes and toys and strollers and diapers. Vishal had not been there with her. He had only been on the periphery. Indulging her, not really participating. She had wondered, then, what sort of father he would be. Not a participative one, she feared. She could imagine months and years of being her child's only real parent, with Vishal joining in to play now and then.

And on the seventeenth day, just the day before she had to do her pregnancy test—she had already bought the test kit—her period started.

* * *

Four years, five IVFs. The doctor had said that they couldn't be closer together, because her body needed time to recover. 'It's the hormones,' she explained, when Kamini went back that first time. 'Because we pump you so full of hormones, your system goes a little haywire. Six months, and you can return.'

Every time, it has been the same. Every time, she has gone through the same procedure. It has become so that she knows the process inside-out, backwards and forwards. She knows which injections are to be administered when, which are intramuscular and which subdermal. Which tests come when, what the results mean or do not mean. She knows what she must do and what she must avoid. She has tried everything to help, from Ayurveda to acupuncture to homoeopathy. She has even let Ma bring a bedsheet— 'My guruji has blessed this himself, it will ensure you conceive'—and cover her with it while she's recovering from the procedure. She has reached the point of no return. If anything works, it is well and good.

At one time, she had ached for this child. When, those first three times she went through the IVF, and she had thought she was finally going to be a mother. Perhaps that hope had given rise to some form of maternal feeling in her. Perhaps the anticipation had been enough to make her feel motherly, to rest her hand protectively on a womb that was, in reality, empty.

Now she goes along with it, going religiously through the regime, following every step, ticking every box. She feels nothing.

No, she thinks as she bends down to caress a glossy leaf of one of the monsteras. No, the fact is that she *does* feel something. She feels a strong loathing for this child that may come. She does not want it. The ache for it has turned into revulsion, because the trying has caused her more anguish, more turmoil than she has ever imagined herself capable of enduring. Every time, each time, it is the same: the increasingly fragile control over her emotions, the hope, the thought that this time she will succeed. The agony, the almost physical pain, when she discovers, once again, that she has failed. She has failed, even though the doctor says there is nothing wrong with her. She hates this child-to-be, or not-to-be, with all her heart.

Yet she cannot bring herself to say no, to put a stop to further trying.

But it is your body, she tells herself. Your decision.

Is it? She knows Ma will be furious if Kamini refuses to keep trying until the end of time. And Vishal will say, 'Why did you give up your job and concentrate on having a baby, then? And what have we spent so much money on, all these years? So many lakhs, gone down the drain? Just because you've given up?' Her parents, though they say nothing, will be disappointed. Friends, colleagues, everybody she knows who has children—and who know nothing of what she has gone through, these past years—will continue to stare at her with a mixture of pity and derision. Poor, childless Kamini.

The phone rings. She ignores it. It is probably a telemarketer. It stops after about half a minute. Then, just as she relaxes, it starts again. Again and again, until she gets so sick of it that she gets up and goes to it. It is Vishal's number, she sees. Why would he be calling? He rarely calls when he's out of town, unless there's something urgent.

'Hmm?'

'Hello? Who's this?' It is a man's voice, a little breathless, nervous. What is a stranger doing with Vishal's phone? Her mind is racing, even as the man begins to introduce himself. She can hear him, but she's not listening, not really. Has something happened to Vishal? Like his brother, has he too died of a heart attack? These things are hereditary, and Vishal is not careful. If he is dead, that will be the end. No obligations. No pressing need to have a baby. No—no nothing. The relief, the euphoria, leaves her so weak that she has to sit down.

'—so I thought I'd call. Your number was saved in the favourites.'

She is light-headed by now as she clutches the phone and wonders what she will do. Go back to work, move into a flat of her own—surely Preeti's landlady still has that two-room set, which was so pleasant but not too expensive? She will not be—

'Kamini?' Vishal's voice, replacing the stranger's. 'Hey, sorry. I forgot my phone at this office. This guy here found it and was trying to figure out who I was. It's fine, no worries.'

Kamini asks him if he's all right, and when he hangs up, she wanders out to the other balcony. The monkeys have arrived. One large male, and a troop of smaller females. Three of them have babies clinging to their backs. They swoop through the mango tree, grabbing at the fruit, sitting on the branches and eating half of one mango before throwing it away and snatching another. They squabble.

The male catches a glimpse of her, looking out at them from behind the two doors, and it snarls.

Suddenly, she is flinging open the doors. First the glass-paned one, then the grille. Snatching up the heavy stick that leans against the wall, just in case one gets caught out on the balcony when the monkeys are around. Up, and at them. She screams, a harsh cry of anguish and despair. Again and again, as she lashes out wildly. The male leaps forward, but a blow from the stick hits him and he retreats, snarling and spitting. The monkeys flee, thrashing through the branches of the tree.

Kamini sinks down onto the floor and weeps.

Maplewood

THIS HOUSE REEKS of viciousness. It hates me. I can tell. It wants me out of here. For Maplewood, I am an interloper. It hems me in, trying to suffocate me with its closeness. A malevolent closeness, not a loving embrace. As if it wanted to squeeze the life out of me. The windows are too few and too small. The rooms are too dark, the verandas beyond too close to the trees that surround the house.

I wish there were no trees here. I had read somewhere that colonial bungalows were designed to sit, grand and isolated, in large compounds. Sweeping driveways and neat squares or rectangles of neatly clipped lawn. The odd tree here and there, providing shade for the memsahib and the sahib when they chose to go for a stroll or to take tea under the trees, as the fancy took them.

No other bungalows I have seen have trees like this, coming right up to the house, trying to draw it into themselves. At night, lying awake in my bed, I can hear the rustle of leaves brushing against the chhajjas, the overhangs of the roof. I can hear odd noises—'Owls copulating,' my son said, when I told him. 'You have a vivid imagination, Ma. Don't get carried away.'

But sometimes I feel Maplewood will carry me away, not by my imagination, but by its trees. When there is a storm, the trees howl and shriek and blow in the wind, as if they want to carry Maplewood away with them, far away from this quiet little part of the world.

Where will they take it, I wonder? To some obscure little corner of England? A place of rolling meadows and cottonwool clouds and cattle peacefully grazing? Was that the place the man who built this house hailed from? Or was he a city man? Someone, perhaps, from out of one of Dickens's books. A man who had grown up in the squalor and stink of the seedier parts of London, but—like David Copperfield or Oliver Twist—had risen in life. A civil servant, I thought, a man who had come out East and made his fortune. But a man who had spent enough of his life in the close confines of East London to feel vulnerable in the wide open spaces. Perhaps this suffocating closeness, the trees hugging the bungalow, had been an attempt to replicate that atmosphere.

I don't know what that long-ago man looked like. Is he the short, bearded man in a white suit who peers out from behind round spectacles in that yellowed photograph on the mantelpiece? Or the taller, broader man, standing in dress uniform in a studio, his hand resting on the hilt of a sword? Or the pixie-like man who sits sprawling in a garden chair? Is it one of the many people—each of them alone, staring in solitary splendour out of their picture frames—whose photos inhabit Maplewood?

Who knows. This house is full of photographs. Photographs that have been left behind, forgotten by those who they should have kept alive for all eternity. Or at least as long as the photos survived.

I found the photographs when I first arrived in Maplewood. At first, it was exciting to unearth the past of

Maplewood. I went through old trunks and chests, racks of mouldy and dusty books. I would find one photo, then another—sometimes of the same person, at a different stage in life: older, more weatherworn, more calloused, perhaps. But I could never find names to any of them.

I've never even been able to find evidence of the name for the house I live in. There is no sign outside, no plaque, no anything that stamps this bungalow as Maplewood. My husband Vivek had told me it was called Maplewood, and I never questioned that. Even though this is not a land of maples. There are sal trees. There are sheeshams and mangoes, a couple of guava trees. But no maples. Of course not.

Vivek inherited it from an old bachelor uncle—a man more wealthy than wise—who had bought it at an auction after the death of its last occupant, an old English clergyman who had stayed on in India after Independence. Why, we did not know. How he happened to own Maplewood, we did not know. But when he died, Vivek's uncle bid for Maplewood—and got it. He never lived here, except for a week shortly after it became his. 'Just to get the feel of it,' he had said.

He willed it to Vivek, and Vivek never lived in it. He did not like it. Vivek was a city man, a man who hated to be too far from all the conveniences of urban life. For the sake of it, and to see his inheritance, we had come here once. Vivek had had one look around the house, and had refused to spend a single night here. 'It's the boondocks, this place. Let's go,' he had said. Maplewood sits just inside Madhya Pradesh, near its border with Maharashtra, and I remember it took us many hours to drive all the way back to Mumbai. A wasted trip, Vivek had said with disgust.

Now that Vivek is gone, Maplewood has come to me. I had no place to go; the rented flat in Mumbai was too expensive for me to afford on my own. And Maplewood, standing here in the back of beyond, stood vacant. 'It's the best place for you to stay,' my son said. 'Nice and quiet. None of the mad hustle and bustle of the city.' He had paused and looked a little worried as he added, 'You wouldn't want to stay with me, would you?'

I couldn't say so. Not after the nervous way in which he had said it.

Yes, it is quiet. It is laidback. The nearest shop is in the village, two kilometres down a dirt road. The village itself is hardly a coherent settlement: more a loosely connected bunch of huts and sheds, scattered across many acres. There are fields, and one mango plantation. The richest man—the one who owns the plantation—is the owner of the shop. I have seen him once, when my son first drove me here. Since then, I have not gone to the village; Meena, who looks after the house, buys for me whatever I need and runs my errands. She is my conduit to the world outside. I feel no need to step out: I am nervous, too, I suppose. Shy and a little scared of what may lie outside these walls. Mumbai I knew well; this sleepy stretch of countryside is new and mysterious enough to intimidate me. I have remained inside Maplewood.

The village comes to me, though, now and then.

Last night it did.

The monsoon is here, and the earth barely has time to dry after a shower before the clouds gather again. Last evening, the sky was so grey and oppressive that I retreated from the veranda—the only place with any appreciable natural light—and went into the drawing room. Maplewood has electricity, but it is erratic. Yesterday there was none.

Meena lit a lantern and brought it into the drawing room. 'I have made your dinner, memsahib,' she said. 'I've left it on the kitchen counter.' She hesitated, as if reluctant to go on. She is a conscientious girl; I pay her for eight hours' work daily, and she will not leave before those eight hours are over, not even if she really has nothing else to do.

After a few moments of silence, she put the lantern down on the little table beside my rocking chair and said, 'I need to go now, memsahib. Before the rain comes.'

Meena must have got caught in the rain after all, I thought later. It began just minutes after she had gone. The first drops were fat and lazy, as if still wondering whether they should take the trouble of visiting Maplewood. Then, suddenly, the rain changed to a flurry—a mad, violent assault on the house. Heavy, fast-falling drops clattered against the roof. Lightning flashed, thunder rattled the windowpanes. The trees fought back. Maplewood battled the elements, and I gripped the arms of my rocking chair and sat up straight and rigid, with my eyes closed.

I came awake sometime in the depths of the night, the sound of loud knocking still echoing in my head. My head throbbed, my throat was parched and my stomach complained because I had fallen asleep without dinner.

Someone was knocking—no, not even knocking, *banging*—at the door.

I called, asking who it was. There was no reply; perhaps my voice, a tremulous croak even to my own ears, was too low to be heard through the thick planks of the door. Perhaps the thunder and the rain drowned out every other sound. I got to my feet and padded across to peer out of the window next to the door.

It was a thin woman, her half-sari gleaming white under

the enormous black umbrella she was holding. Even though she was standing in the veranda. I did not recognize her—I couldn't see her face—but I stepped across to the door and opened it.

It was Gunvanti—I recognized her as soon as she said, 'Baisahib.' I knew very few of the women from the village; this was one I did know, the only one who called me baisahib, rather than memsahib. I had never asked her why. She was old enough to have been around when Maplewood still had its sahibs and memsahibs. Perhaps she thought 'memsahib' should be reserved for a white-skinned lady in dresses, wearing hats and high heels. Not a brown-skinned frump in a crumpled sari. For Gunvanti, 'baisahib' was all the respect I was entitled to.

Her bare feet were wet and muddy, but otherwise, she was all right. She put her umbrella down on the veranda and stepped up to the threshold, blinking in the light from the lantern. 'Is Meena here, baisahib?'

Belatedly, I remembered that Gunvanti was related in some roundabout way to Meena. Meena's mother-in-law? Grandaunt? Aunt-in-law? I wasn't sure.

I shook my head. 'She left. Just before the rain started. Why? Isn't she home yet?' There was a sudden clap of thunder and both of us jumped. I beckoned to her to come in.

'I don't know,' Gunvanti said. 'I haven't come from home. I was across the village, at Bhavani's house. His wife was having a baby.'

I had forgotten Gunvanti was the local midwife. Someone had told me once. Perhaps it had been Meena, in one of her more chatty moments as she went about her work.

I sat down in my rocking chair again, and gestured to

Gunvanti to sit. She did, on her haunches opposite me, gathering up the edges of her sari around her thighs. A scrawny but strong woman, perhaps as old as me, but with her hair just beginning to turn grey. Not more salt than pepper, like mine. I asked her if she wanted tea, or something to eat. She shook her head. 'Bhavani's sister made tea for me. And I'm not hungry.' She rummaged about in the folds of her sari around her waist, and drew forth something—I couldn't see what. 'I'll have a beedi, instead,' she said.

I had not expected her to ask me politely if I minded her smoking, but the matter-of-fact way in which she made herself at home startled me. She got up, went to the lantern, and lit her beedi from it.

I sat, stiff with indignation—I hate that pungent, all-pervasive smell of beedis—but I did not say anything. The flame in the lantern sprang up merrily, as if it rejoiced at my discomfort, when Gunvanti stepped back.

This house hates me. The furniture, the carpets, the clock on the wall, the lantern—everything that came with the house—hates me.

Gunvanti settled herself back on the floor, pulling contentedly at her beedi. 'It was an easy birth,' she said. 'Her second. The first one was bad. Bad for her, bad for me, bad for the baby. But we made it through that one, too.' She held the beedi cupped in one hand and peered at it for half a minute. Then she looked up at me. 'What about you, baisahib? You have a son, don't you?'

I nodded.

'Good. Any other children? More sons? Daughters?'

I shook my head.

'Your son lives in the city, baisahib? He came here two

years ago, didn't he? When you first moved into Maplood?'
None of the villagers could pronounce Maplewood.

'Yes,' I said.

'He has not come since?'

'He is a busy man.'

'What does he do, baisahib?'

How did one say 'software engineer' in a way that
would make sense to someone like Gunvanti? Even I wasn't
sure exactly what it meant, but I knew it was something
to do with computers. 'Important things,' I said finally.
'Things that help the city run.'

She looked up at me, puzzlement in her eyes. But
when you've lived as long as I have—as Gunvanti has—
you instinctively understand which questions will not be
answered any further. You understand which questions
cannot be answered. And you keep quiet, as she did.

Another puff at her beedi, a dry cough. Then she asked,
'He is married?'

'Not yet.'

'Hmm. And still he does not have the time to come and
see you? How does he know whether you're well or not?
Whether you need anything?'

I remained silent. What could I say? No? Yes? But no to
what? Yes to what? Would I say yes, he knew? No, he didn't
know? Or no, I hadn't told him? Or—the truth—which he
had not guessed? Or, if he had guessed, that he did not have
the time to think about it. How this house threatened me,
suffocated me. And that I loved him too much to want to
be a burden on him. Not monetarily, that much I was sure
of. But emotionally I did not want him thinking of me as
demanding.

'We talk on the phone sometimes,' I said.

She did not comment on that. All she did was give a lopsided smirk. As if she knew that was only part of the truth. Meena, chatting with Gunvanti, would probably have mentioned it. Meena, who would be around the house, sweeping the floor or mopping it at noon every Saturday when my son phoned. They would have shaken their heads about it, tut-tutted over this pathetic old woman who would be sitting next to the phone from ten in the morning, just waiting for it to ring. How she would pick it up as soon as it rang, even in mid-ring. And how short the conversation would be. A quick how-are-you and what's-new. A polite, hurried conversation because one of the two people in it was eager to hurry on with life.

This conversation with Gunvanti, I thought, was the longest I'd had with anyone since the day I'd moved into Maplewood, so much so that I did not find her curiosity any more out of place or odd than my making small talk.

'There are no others?' Gunvanti persisted. 'You have no other relatives? No brothers? Sisters? Cousins? Nieces? Nephews? People on your man's side?'

I mentally ran over the list of people who had once existed in my life. I had had no siblings. Yes, there had been cousins, five of them in all, on both my mother and father's side. Our families were small. Perhaps our parents were progressive and in favour of population control way back then, when it wasn't a big deal to have a horde of children. Or perhaps our parents just weren't too interested in procreation or what went into it.

My cousins had had children. But it's easy to drift apart, especially when everybody has their own life to live. Vivek had had a brother—dead seven years now from a very quick and sudden heart attack—and a sister.

'My husband's sister is alive,' I replied. 'She lives very far away.' And we never did like each other much, I added to myself. While Vivek was alive, there had been the occasional phone call—at Diwali, or on her birthday. But when Vivek died, that ended too. Her last phone call had come three years ago, when I was still in Mumbai. My son had phoned to let her know of Vivek's death, and she had asked to speak to me. 'You know it will be impossible for me to get back to India in time for the cremation,' she had said. 'But I'm sorry. You know that.'

As if she had not lost a brother as much as I had a husband.

Gunvanti stood up, her hand resting briefly on one knee as she unbent herself. She went to the cold, long-unused fireplace and stubbed the remains of her beedi into it. I watched her as she stood there, one bare foot resting on the stone grate around the fireplace, one hand clinging to the mantelpiece. She stared into the fireplace—white-painted now, not blackened with soot, as it must have once been—and then, just as I was about to ask her if she was all right, she straightened.

'You should—' she began to say, but she was interrupted in mid-sentence. From outside, cutting through the sound of rain and thunder and wind, came the muffled shouting of a man. I couldn't understand what he was saying, but it was one word. The same word, repeated over and over, at brief intervals. As if he were searching for someone, calling and then waiting to hear an answering call, before calling again.

Gunvanti bustled away towards the door. She looked over her shoulder just as she reached the door, to say, 'It's my nephew. I'll let him know I'm here.' She swung one leaf of the door open, passed through and tugged the door shut behind her. Even then, a gust of wind brought in enough water to wet the floor.

I sat in my chair, rocking slowly to and fro, straining to hear anything other than the storm outside. Who was this nephew? What was his name? What had made him come to Maplewood?

Would someone come to Maplewood someday, calling for me?

I tried to push the thought out of my mind. It was stupid, weak. *I was a strong woman.* I had always prided myself on my willpower, my ability to not crumble. I had worked through all the years between graduating from college, all the way till when Vivek had died. I had juggled home and hearth in a day and age when we didn't have washing machines and microwave ovens, and in dire times when we couldn't even afford a maid. I had put a brave smile on my face and said, 'It doesn't matter, I will manage.'

And I had. Managed well and proper, till the point where I was left alone with only the storm howling outside for company. And a village midwife who had taken refuge in this house.

The door opened again, and Gunvanti stumbled in, wiping rainwater off her face. She pushed the door shut behind her, and went back to stand next to the fireplace. That pensive look had gone; she was grinning now, chuckling as she squeezed the end of her cotton sari into the fireplace. 'These children,' she said, wagging her head. 'How they worry!'

She stretched out her arms, spreading the thin cloth, flapping it about so that it would dry. It won't, I wanted to tell her. Nothing dries in this house. It just stays in the air, mouldering and seeping into the fabric of Maplewood.

She turned to look over one bony shoulder at me. 'That was Gokul, Bhavani's wife's younger brother.'

She must have noticed the puzzlement on my face. 'Bhavani. The man whose wife just had a child.'

I nodded.

'He came to check if I had reached home all right. Bhavani was very sorry, he said, that he'd been so caught up in admiring his child that he never even realized when I left.' The grin grew wider. I could almost see Gunvanti preening herself as she draped the still-damp end of the sari back over her shoulder and around her skinny waist, tucking it into her side.

'But you haven't gone home,' I said, my voice sounding loud and unnatural in the room.

'Hmm.' She lowered herself onto the floor. 'Gokul went to my hut to check. When Meena told him I hadn't come back, he went searching for me. He'd been searching this past half hour.'

'You should have told him to come in,' I said. 'Where is he? Has he gone back home?'

She nodded, yes. 'But he'll be back. He said he'll return once it stops raining.'

We sat there in that high-ceilinged room, two old women. One damp and thin and hungry—I had asked her again if she wanted tea or food, but Gunvanti had refused—but contented. The other dry and comfortable and jealous. *Immeasurably jealous.* I envied Gunvanti the people who surrounded her. The people who needed her, cared for her. The young man who had walked through torrential rain to look for her. The man who had sent him, who had apologized for being too caught up in his own new child. The child she had helped bring into this world. The child's mother. The child's sibling, who had been through a difficult birth but had lived.

And what about the child *you* brought into this world, Maplewood asked, in a malicious whisper. What about him? Does he care for you? Does anybody care for you?

I don't know when I nodded off. I had been sitting, chin resting on my chest, rocking gently in my chair one moment. The next, I was awake, and instead of the warm yellow glow of the lantern, there was the gloomy grey of the dawn filtering in through the thick wire mesh of the windows. Instead of the thunder and the incessant weeping of the skies, there was silence. Or almost silence—somewhere far away I could hear a crow cawing.

There was no one in the room. Sometime during the night, the storm must have stopped. Gokul must have come and taken Gunvanti back to her home.

Home.

I was home.

Or was I?

I sat in the rocking chair, staring at my lap. The pendulum clock on the wall counted out the seconds in loud, precise ticks.

One teardrop made its way down my cheek. It hung for a long moment from my jaw, and then dripped onto my hand.

I sat there, listening to the clock, watching my tears drip into my hands and soak into the wrinkles of my sari. When I finally straightened, it was to look up at the ceiling, at the fan that hung there. Like all that is in Maplewood, this is a fan of colonial days. The rod that attaches it to the ceiling is a heavy iron one. The fan itself is a heavy one, slow-moving and majestic. Well able to take my weight.

Meena will come, perhaps in an hour or two. She will be upset. Perhaps she will scream. Or, sensible girl that she is, she will probably run straight back to the village to fetch some of the men. Gokul will be shocked. Gunvanti will perhaps remember snatches of our conversation. They will wonder why the memsahib, living all grand and alone in that big beautiful bungalow, resorted to this.

But there are, finally, people around me. They smile at me. The man with the beard and the round glasses, the pixie-like fellow, even the supercilious officer—his eyes do not smile, but he nods at me. An old man, in vestments. A woman with a bustle and a beautiful hat, her eyes sad. She has blue eyes, not the bleak brown of the sepia portrait on the shelf.

There are others, people I have never known by name, but whom I am familiar with, coming forward to me, reaching out, welcoming me into their midst.

They are Maplewood.

And finally, I am, too.

I am home.

Captive Spirit

LALA GULABCHAND'S FATHER had built the haveli in Dharampura some time in the 1860s. It was a fine haveli, its gate carved in a mass of flowers and birds, each of its four courtyards spacious enough to host a gathering of fifty guests for one of Lalaji's exclusive mushairas. Chandni Chowk was a hop, skip and jump away, Daryaganj, where Lalaji conducted much of his trade—in textile—was an easy ride by tonga. Or, by the time Gulabchand had taken over the title of Lalaji after the old man's death, an easy ride in the phaeton. True, Gulabchand was not Chunnamal, who had owned Delhi's first car, or whose haveli had been the first in Delhi to get its own telephone, but he was, in his own realm, a man much respected.

A man, too, who—from the day he got married—began planning the expansion of his business and his haveli. He would have many sons and daughters, Gulabchand had decided. Sons to carry on the business, daughters to marry into other influential families and forge ties. Within a month of being married, Gulabchand had begun negotiations to buy the havelis on either side of his own. Within six months, he had bought them and had employed an architect.

Ten years later, with the haveli now a sprawl of rooms

and courtyards, Gulabchand had to regretfully admit to himself that he had perhaps been a trifle premature. His wife had died in childbirth, her baby with her. His second wife, married a year later, had so far given him no offspring. The haveli, instead of ringing with childish laughter and the patter of little feet, sat solemn and lonely. All his plans had gone to waste.

And so it continued till 1899, by which time his wife Ratnamala, now nearly thirty-five years old, had resigned herself to the sly taunts, the sighs and reproaches of family, neighbours and acquaintances. An old aunt had tactlessly suggested that Gulabchand take another wife. Someone else had concocted—and had the insensitivity to divulge it to Ratnamala—a complex plan involving a healthy maid, a quiet night, some surreptitious smuggling away into the hills 'if all went well', and the subsequent triumphant return, babe in arms, to Dilli.

Ratnamala surprised them all, herself included, by becoming pregnant in the last year of the century. Laxmi was born in March 1900, and a beautiful baby she was. Beautiful, and pampered, the darling of the Dharampura haveli. When she cried, a platoon of servants would come running. When she sat up for the first time, Lala Gulabchand had a servant take the phaeton and hurry to fetch the nearest photographer. He gifted Laxmi, on her first birthday, with not just the expected English doll (hat, gowns and tiny diamond necklace included), but a little jewellery box as well. A sandook, already with its inaugural pair of gold bangles, a necklace and paayals.

Into that jewellery box, on each of Laxmi's subsequent birthdays, went her gifts. From, sometimes, the grudging relative who had been harbouring now-dashed hopes of inheriting Lalaji's wealth. Sometimes from the wives of Gulabchand's associates, women who had been sent with strict instructions by husbands who had discovered that Gulabchand loved Laxmi to distraction. And that Laxmi, whose dearest possession was that little sandook of hers, could—just by mentioning a name—convince her father that so-and-so benefactor was the best person in the world.

And so it went on. Laxmi was admitted to the Indraprastha Girls' School and went there, reluctantly, in a closed palanquin every day. To sit brooding at the back of the classroom, paying little attention to anything, and waiting always for the day to end, so that she could go home to her expensive doll and her sandook. A friend, wide-eyed with awe, would occasionally be invited home. Laxmi liked to see the reaction when the doll—named Missie Sahib—was taken out, dressed in blue satin, with the diamonds twinkling around her neck. Or when Laxmi showed off her own earrings, her necklaces, her bangles and bracelets and whatnot.

When she was fifteen, Laxmi came home one day to overhear her mother telling a visitor that Lalaji had found a brilliant match for Laxmi. A young man who worked as a printer, but who was destined for far greater things. And who belonged, moreover, to one of the city's oldest and most respected families. A son-in-law Lalaji could not wait to welcome into the family.

Laxmi did not wait, either. She marched into the room and said to Ratnamala—in the presence of the woman who had come visiting—'If I am to get married, why should I have to go to school any more? Can I not leave? I will need to prepare to be a bride. If I stay at home and study diligently to be a good wife, that will be far better, will it not?'

And so Laxmi left school and married my mother's granduncle.

* * *

The photo lies in the back of my parents' wedding album. It's an old album, dating back to the 1960s. Padded cover, onionskin leaves separating one thick black page from the next. Little hinges of silver foil frame each black-and-white photo. There are photos, of course, of my parents being married. Of my mother, demure and shy like I have never seen her. Of my father, looking inordinately pleased with himself. After the last photo—of the two families all together, fifty-odd people strong—there are isolated photos to fill up the album. Photos of Ma during their honeymoon in Shimla. A family picnic, with all Ma's cousins and uncles and aunts.

And, in a large but fragile brown envelope, some photos from around the turn of the century. Nothing very inspiring: someone's grandfather, looking rather like Swami Vivekanand, turban and crossed arms included. A little boy dressed up in dhoti and kurta. Two little girls wearing frocks, their eyes lined with kaajal.

Laxmi.

Hers is the one photo that stands out. It shows its age, like the others—its black faded to sepia, its white yellowed. But, unlike the others, it holds your attention. She is a young woman in a posed shot. A studio portrait. She stands there, beside what used to be called an occasional table. The table is tall, and on it, beside a vase of flowers, rests her right hand. Her other arm hangs by her side. Her gaze, level and bold, holds the camera. 'You had to stand very still back then,' Ma says. But Laxmi doesn't look as if she's been told to stand still. She looks as if she's been requested to stand still, and has deigned to do so. There's a difference.

She's thin, her elbows sharp, the bones of her face angular. Her lips are full, the bindi on her forehead the size, almost, of a small lime. And those eyes. Large. Fearless. Self-assured.

I see all of that now. When I first saw Laxmi's photo, when I was eight and looking through Ma and Papa's wedding album for the first time, what I saw was not so much the young woman but the jewellery she wore. Even though I could not see the yellow of the gold or the colours of the precious stones, it took my breath away.

She wears—I counted them, again and again, that first time—seven necklaces about her neck, all the way from a choker studded with huge baguette-shaped stones, to a long chain with a massive pendant that hangs down to well below her bosom. Around her narrow waist is a broad belt crafted from metallic flowers, little loops of gleaming chains connecting one calyx to the other. A maang teeka trails down the parting of her hair, the round pendant of it resting on her forehead. There is a nose-ring, an ostentatious one, covering part of one cheek and resting on the curve of her upper lip. The sari has its embroidered zari, but that is reduced to a mere shadow of what it might be because of the ornaments.

Yes, there are more. Toe-rings on her feet, heavy anklets that peep under the brocade hem of the sari. Jhumkas, chandelier-shaped earrings, that hang from her ears. Rings, a total of five of them spread across both hands. And bangles. So many bangles, glittering and gleaming, broad and narrow, that they mount right up to her elbow. At the wrists are a matching pair of bracelets. They are an unusual pattern, a row of lilies made of filigree, with a very thin band of seed pearls on either edge. The pearls are white, and there are more of them on the inside of each lily, forming stamens.

That detail cannot be seen in the photo, of course, but I know. I know, just as I know that the gold is the deep, rich colour of mellow honey, the sort of gold you don't see these days. Old gold. Old but beautiful pearls. I know, because Ma has one of those bracelets. I saw it one day, years and years ago, when I was sixteen and Ma was getting ready for a party. She had worn her peach chiffon with the silver border and was busy pinning up her bun when she called over her shoulder, 'Meenu, open my jewellery drawer and take out my silver earrings, will you? And the bangles that go with them.' Ma didn't need to explain further. She didn't have much jewellery, not because she couldn't afford it, but because she has never really been interested in it. Neither am I.

That evening, scrabbling about in Ma's jewellery drawer, I stumbled across, right at the back of the drawer, an old box I had never seen before. It was covered in deep blue velvet, old but not worn. Even though I had already found what Ma needed, I opened the box, curious. In it was that bracelet. So lovely, so heavy yet so delicate. I gaped at it. 'Ma,' I said, hurrying to her—she was reaching out to pick up her lipstick—'why do you never wear this? It's so beautiful!'

I have only read in books about people turning pale. I had never seen it happen in real life. That evening, I saw Ma go very white.

She froze, one arm raised, with the lipstick half-emerged

from the golden tube in which it nested. 'Put that back, Meenu,' she said in a quiet voice. A voice that shook. 'Why did you take it out? Put it back.'

'But, Ma. Why don't you wear it? It's—'

For a moment Ma looked as if she would hit me. But she took a deep breath and simply repeated what she had said, her voice even lower, even slower this time. More dangerous. I closed the box on the bracelet and put it away. I wondered, though, why Ma had reacted the way she did. I was not to know, then, because Ma was busy dabbing attar on her wrists, calling to Papa to say she was ready and had he put on his tie?

**

Lala Gulabchand and Ratnamala had started, like all good Indian parents of that time, to build Laxmi's dowry and trousseau almost from the day she was born. Carved furniture, teak and Indian rosewood inlaid with mother-of-pearl and ivory. Pots and pans, fine porcelain all the way from Europe. Carpets. Trunks full of silks and velvets, the best pashmina and the flimsiest of muslins.

None of these were of much interest to Laxmi, not even when she was told that she had been formally engaged to Mahendranath. In fact, the bulk of the shagun—the 'auspicious gifts' received from her fiancé's household as a token of the betrothal—attracted not much more than a fleeting glance from her. The laddoos and pedas she ignored, the rich blue Banarasi sari with its gold zari only slightly less. The only things she had eyes for were the necklace with its earrings. She examined them carefully, running the tiny gold beads of the necklace through her fingers, checking them for unevenness. Peering at them—and at the delicate filigree of the pendant and its matching earrings—through her father's magnifying glass. Looking up with a smile of satisfaction. 'They are good,' she told her mother.

And, unsurprisingly, it was the jewellery, of all her trousseau, that she was interested in. Ratnamala was allowed to buy whatever saris and shawls and imported coats and stoles she liked but Laxmi did not show the slightest inclination to even get into the new car and go shopping for those. When the servants brought in Ratnamala's purchases and Ratnamala tried to show off what she had bought, Laxmi would harrumph and leave after a minute or two of cursory perusal.

For her jewellery, however, she insisted on being taken along. Only fifteen, but she knew what she wanted. Knew, from numerous questions posed to mother and aunts and grandmothers over the years, what was good and what was not. Knew how to tell a real diamond from an artificial one. Knew which gemstones suited her. Could tell whether the enamel on the bangle she was being shown would last a lifetime or two weeks.

That photograph of hers, that one of Laxmi bedecked in a king's ransom of jewellery, dates from 1916. She had been married a year, and Mahendranath—whose elder brother, Surendranath, was my mother's grandfather—was both in love with her, and a little in awe of her. He was five years older than her, a conscientious young man who had been working at the printer's for the past four years. He was quiet and studious, happiest when he was in his modest library at home. His books, and his work: those were his greatest passions in life. Secretly, perhaps, he had hoped for a wife who could also become a passion, but Laxmi was too different from him, and too unmindful of his ways. They were not really compatible, but as was common back then, it hardly mattered. He learnt, quickly enough, to live with her.

Everybody did, even if she unsettled them. There was something about her that was disquieting. That self-assured gaze, perhaps. Or her fearlessness, her lack of concern for what she said and to whom. Most of all, it was that odd obsession with her jewellery.

* * *

'My mother told me most of this,' Ma said, when she told me the story.

I was about nineteen years old, rehearsing the part of Vasantsena for a college drama production of *Mrichhakatika*. I had been provided with costume jewellery, but all of it looked so tawdry that I was certain I'd get booed off the stage. I remembered, then, that bracelet lying in that forgotten box at the back of Ma's jewellery drawer. Ma refused to let me have it. 'It's gold,' she said. 'What if you lost it? I know how absent-minded you are. And the confusion backstage: no wonder you're given costume jewellery.'

I could tell she was reluctant to have me wear it, and in my frustration, I burst out, 'Why this dog in the manger attitude, Ma? You refuse to wear it, and you won't let me wear it, either. Why? What is so special about this stupid bloody bracelet?'

So she told me. That warm, sticky day in August, with storm clouds turning the sky the colour of iron, Ma sat me down with two big mugs of coffee, and told me. It was the first time she'd let me have coffee at home—'too much caffeine,' was what she'd always said, 'you're too young.' That day, I think, she decided I wasn't too young any more.

'I was about your age when Laxmi died,' Ma said. 'I knew her only in the later years of her life. But my mother told me all about her, after she had died.' She sipped her coffee. 'As she was dying.'

She glanced up, noticed the look on my face, the incomprehension. 'Laxmi took a long time dying,' she explained.

But she told me first, not of how Laxmi died, but of how she lived.

For her jewellery.

It was not as if Laxmi was selfish or cold-hearted or mercenary. She was not. She was well-liked in society. People praised her for being a gracious hostess, a charming woman. She was no less and no more considerate to the poor and needy than others of her class. Aware of her wealth and status (or the wealth and status, really, of first her father and later her husband) to let the sheen show, but not preening.

Unlike her mother, Laxmi turned out to be blessedly fecund. Within five years of marriage, she had given Mahendra three strong and healthy sons. Good boys, said everybody, and it was obvious to all that Laxmi loved them dearly. Not, perhaps, with the blind devotion people seem to expect of mothers, but well enough.

Yet, there was always that something that niggled. Something that made people frown and whisper behind her back. The time when her eldest, then four years old, had come limping in, blood streaming from a cut knee and cheeks wet with tears. One of Laxmi's favourite jewellers from Dariba was in the drawing room, and Laxmi sat amidst a dozen boxes, some open, others still shut. Pearls, gold, diamonds and rubies glittered on velvet and silk. On her neck and hands and in her ears.

'Ma!' Mohan sobbed, hobbling his way to her. 'Ma! I fell down. There was this stone—'

'Yes, it's bad, isn't it? My poor child,' Laxmi had said, casting a glance at the wounded knee and making a moue of commiseration. 'Go to your ayah. She'll clean it up and bandage it.' She patted him on the shoulder with a hand heavy with rings. 'Watch where you're going, beta. Don't drip blood on those pretty jewels.'

Those were the years of the Indian freedom movement, of course, and there were upheavals now and then. Party workers and others purporting to be party workers used to come by, exhorting the wealthy to give for the nation. Nobody ever asked them who they were—mostly, people didn't even know whether these were Congress or Communists or Muslim League or just a bunch of young men trying to make an easy buck—and their reception differed from one household to the next. Some gave. Some held back. Some, like the ageing Lala Gulabchand in his Dharampura haveli, gave generously. Others, like his beautiful daughter, sniffed in disdain, affixed a jewelled pin to the shoulder of her sari, and said, 'We have done our bit.' And she had: she had given a full hundred rupees—a lot in that day and age. Perhaps not, though, for someone who spent more than five times that sum on a ring.

This, though, was only the start of it. The movement was to pick up pace, and—as the years passed and yet another war began—things began to take a turn for the worse. Laxmi and her family, both the one she had been born in and the one she had married into, were too wealthy, too well-connected and too confident of their positions in society to worry about such mundane things as food shortages and the like. Yes, said Laxmi when a group of socially-minded women came to call, collecting blankets for the poor and asking for things to be sent to our soldiers overseas. It was too bad that so many were dying. She gave them money, she promised to send one of her servants with woollens and blankets.

'She sounds odd,' I remarked, when Ma told me this.

'Just human.' Ma put down the mug of coffee she had been sipping from, and looked me in the eye. 'Laxmi was no saint, and she was no villain, either. Just human in most ways. Normal, everyday people don't give away all they possess for the poor. And they don't deliberately go out to victimize the poor either. Nobody is all good or all bad. The world is greys, not pitch-black or snowwhite.'

But there was that obsession of Laxmi's, that somewhat unearthly love for her jewellery. When her eldest son got married in December 1942—in the middle of the war, when there were cries and pleas for austerity ringing in the air— Laxmi agreed to comply. Only a very few, very select guests were invited for the wedding. The food was simple: rice, chappati, dal, two types of vegetable, kheer to finish. The bride was given, by her new mother-in-law, no more than three silk saris and a simple gold necklace with matching earrings.

Some of the more judgemental guests, most of them female relatives, confessed to being surprised at Laxmi's own appearance. The sari she wore was a rich one, a peacock blue Banarasi with gold zari—but all she wore in the way of jewellery was a single pair of gold jhumkas in her ears. Small jhumkas too, unostentatious and almost not there, by Laxmi's standards.

They could not see beneath the voluminous shawl she wore. They had no way of knowing that when she was back in her room, when every last guest had departed and there were no prying eyes to be seen, Laxmi removed her shawl and her cardigan, and stood in front of the tall mirror, admiring the necklaces, the jewelled waistband, the baazubands that encircled her upper arms.

'How do *you* know, Ma?'

'She told my grandmother,' Ma said. 'Later. Several weeks later.' She peered into her coffee mug, swirled it about, and drank down the last swallow. 'My dadi was a sweet soul, you know. Quiet and gentle, never pointing fingers at anyone. She was one of the few people who didn't try to tell Laxmi what to do and what not to do. So Laxmi thought of her as something of a confidante. When she couldn't tell anyone else, she told my dadi.'

Or when there was a delicious little secret, one which might have drawn censure from others. Such as in this instance. Or in more dangerous times, on occasions that were a matter of life and death.

The worst came in 1947. The Partition, with all its turmoil. When their wealth and social standing were no longer a shield against those out to kill. Delhi had erupted into madness, and there were people roaming the streets in packs, armed with everything from sickles to old swords to rifles and daggers. Ready to cut down whoever seemed to not be of their religion.

One night, the family was jolted out of a restless sleep by an uproar outside, in the road. There were women screaming, children crying. Men shouting, someone banging hard on their front door. And, forming a backdrop to all that noise, the roaring of fire. They learnt later that somebody had run through the narrow lane, splashing kerosene on the walls of the houses. Followed closely by another with a blazing torch in hand.

The neighbourhood had come awake in a panic. Most were scurrying about, trying to draw water from wells, urging people to form bucket lines to put out the blaze. Some, realizing perhaps that it was a futile effort, were herding their families together, rushing frantically to gather their belongings and escape. Laxmi's husband and his brother knew, all too soon, that that was what they would have to do too. While the women hurried, collecting their most precious clothes and jewels, the men gathered whatever money was at home, the children their toys...

And then they had all run out onto the main road, clutching their bundles and boxes. Waiting to catch their breath, praying that the fire would by some miracle die down on its own. Or that the firemen would come this way, even though a hundred other fires raged in a dozen other mohallahs. 'Where is Laxmi?' Ma's dadi had suddenly asked, and the panic had arisen, again. The men had put down their loads and gone running back into the house, Mahendra Dada upstairs to where he and Laxmi and their boys had their rooms, his brother—Ma's own grandfather, her dada—into the ground floor. Shouting, with increasing worry, for Laxmi. After a few minutes, worried too for her own husband and his brother, Ma's dadi had sent in a couple of the menservants. And all the while, the fire was drawing closer, the orange of it licking at the boundary wall of the house even though nearly all the servants and other adults of the house had already left their burdens piled beside the gate and were busy trying to put out the fire.

'It took them a full ten minutes to get to Laxmi,' Ma said. 'She was right at the far end of the house, in the kitchen.'

'Picking a forgotten gold earring out of the ashes?' I asked. Of course not, I thought, but I couldn't help myself. What Ma said next, therefore, came as a surprise.

'Not an earring,' she said, with a sigh. 'A ring. A plain gold ring that she used to wear, and which she had taken off while washing her hands. She'd forgotten to put it back on, and realized it was missing only when we were all outside, getting ready to leave.'

And that was how she was. Life did not matter, safety did not matter. Laxmi was surprised, Ma said, when her relatives berated her for having rushed into the house for something so trivial as a ring. Trivial, especially, since all the rest of her jewellery—worth lakhs more than that ring—was already secure. 'But my ring,' she had said, when Mahendra Dada brought her out, looking a little bedraggled—'how could I leave my ring behind? I would never have forgiven myself.'

'Perhaps it had emotional value for her,' I ventured. 'Perhaps there was some attachment to the ring that had nothing to do with its worth in rupees.'

Ma shook her head. 'Nothing of the sort. It had been gifted by somebody—she did not even remember who—at one of those family gatherings, a wedding or something, when everybody's handing out gifts to everybody else. No, Laxmi did not even know who gave it to her. To her, it was only an ornament. The glitter of the gold. That was it.'

Ma closed her eyes and pressed her fingertips to her eyelids, pushing down in that way that always worried me. When I was little, I used to start crying to her to stop before she poked her eyes out. Now, of course, I was old enough to know she wouldn't do anything of the sort, that it was just her way of relieving stress. That when her eyes ached—like they must be now, from staring unblinkingly into the past— she needed to do this. Something like pressing one's palms over one's eyelids, except a little less gentle.

'The bracelet,' she said finally, when she removed her hands from her face and opened her eyes, blinking as she did so. 'You wanted to know about the bracelet.'

Suddenly, I was not so curious any more. Or, to put it differently, I wasn't sure I wanted to know. One part of me did wonder why Ma seemed to find the bracelet— which was beautiful—distasteful. Another part, the one that had started to dislike Laxmi and her obsession with jewellery, guessed that there was something behind that distaste, something that I would not like. I was my mother's daughter, after all.

But I nodded. In a perverse way, I did want to know. Good or bad, knowledge is knowledge.

'She owned the two bracelets from before her wedding,' Ma said. 'They were part of her trousseau.'

'I saw them in the photo. She was wearing them then.'

Ma nodded.

'They were always her favourite,' she said. 'I remember her wearing them at every important family celebration. At weddings. At Diwali. When Mahendra Dada was bestowed some sort of honour by the government, and there was a function. She mellowed with age, I think, because she stopped loading herself down with half her jewellery all at the same time. Perhaps she realized that fashions had changed. Perhaps she realized that wearing a lot of jewellery was passé. Who knows? Even when she stopped wearing those heavy chokers and that waistband and the baazubands, she still wore the bracelets. She loved them.

'She was wearing them that day in 1965, when she slipped in the veranda and fell.' Ma looked out of the window. 'It was a day like this, rain off and on, drippy and damp.'

Laxmi loved the rain, and more than that, the aftermath— the flowers and the leaves all wet and clean, *fresh*. Newly laundered, she would call them. When the rain finally stopped that afternoon, she stepped out onto the veranda and made her way down to where the Rangoon creeper grew, its masses of fragrant pink flowers brushing the railing. The wind had thrown the creeper a little off-kilter and it had swung away from the veranda. Laxmi reached out an arm, tried to touch the flowers. Leaned out a little too far, and slipped. Slipped so badly that she fell, her chin hitting the railing hard enough for the jawbone to shatter, and for the resultant shock to throw her hard onto the stone floor of the veranda.

She was carried back in, concussed and bleeding. The doctor was phoned and came hurrying. Examined her, said that it would be best if she were taken to the hospital.

'Those were his words,' Ma said softly. 'It was not what his eyes said. It was not even what his tone said. Anybody with any experience of life would have realized that he did not expect her to live.'

And Laxmi saw it. Saw it, realized it, and resolutely shook her head—as much as she could—when she was asked if she would let them take her to the hospital. Nobody dared override her wishes, nobody said that no, she would have to be taken to the hospital.

They knew, too. Knew that it would be pointless. And

perhaps somehow humiliating too, for someone like Laxmi, to be looked after by strangers. They nodded to the doctor, and Laxmi's sons ushered him out to ask how she was to be looked after, and what care they were to take of her.

'It is a matter of a day or two,' the doctor said baldly. 'Keep her as comfortable as you can.'

But it turned out to be more than a mere day or two. The women of the house, Laxmi's sister-in-law, Laxmi's three daughters-in-law, even my Ma, who was then still unmarried, took it in turns to sit by her bedside. To wipe her, to make sure she was not too warm and not too cold, to drip water or thin soup or juice into her mouth. To clean her. To read to her, even though Laxmi had never been an avid reader herself, and even though none of them really knew what sort of books she might like read to her.

And Laxmi lay there on her deathbed, staring up at them. Unable to speak, unable to move except to slightly shake her head or flutter her eyelids.

By the end of the second day, it was obvious that she was going. The eyelids had stopped fluttering, the eyes were closed now. Laxmi did not shake her head when anyone asked her if she would like some more juice, or would she like them to read her an excerpt from the *Gita*? (It had been Laxmi's eldest bahu's bright idea that Laxmi's way into the next world be smoothed by having religious scriptures read out to her). Mahendra Dada, who spent at least four hours a day beside his immobile wife's side, came out of the room to mutter to his eldest son: 'Get the Ganga jal. She is fading fast.'

The water of the Ganga, in its little copper vessel, was hurriedly brought, and Mahendra Dada trickled it into Laxmi's mouth. Part of it dripped out of the corner from between her lips, soaking the pillow cover. The entire family, from eldest to youngest, stood solemnly around, watching. Then, when Mahendra Dada had emptied the vessel, they all stepped forward, one by one, to touch the dying woman's feet. To say farewell.

Only she did not die. Not then. Not the next day. Or the next week.

'It was horrible,' Ma said, with a shudder. 'Simply appalling. She just wouldn't die. The breath rattled in her throat, her chest rose and fell. We *knew* she wasn't dead. And yet—yet there was no other sign of life. Her body had begun wasting away in the first couple of days, sagging and wrinkling as if she had aged overnight, but now suddenly it all speeded up. Her skin yellowed, fell back from the sockets of her eyes. Her teeth seemed to jut out, as her lips sank away. She began stinking.' Ma swallowed. 'And then the ants came.'

I stared. I felt sick. That couldn't be true, I thought. It didn't happen that way. It wasn't scientifically possible, was it? That somebody not yet dead could start decomposing?

'Yes,' Ma said, as if I had spoken. 'Yes, we wouldn't have believed it either, if someone had told us that. But we saw. We tried to keep the ants off, brushing them away, stamping at them. Mahendra Dada even sent a servant to bring a chemical to keep the creatures away.' She shook her head. 'But she wouldn't die. It was as if—as if she refused to die.

'We were at the ends of our tethers. It was—well, you can imagine. Ghastly.'

There were furtive discussions, well away from the room, even though they were pretty sure that Laxmi could no longer even perceive their presence. Someone suggested taking her to the hospital anyway: perhaps medical science could provide a quick and painless release for the nightmare they found themselves in. Someone else, less gentle or more frustrated, said, 'Let us take her to Nigambodh Ghat at night and leave her there. They'll attend to her.'

And then, an elderly neighbour—a woman who had known Laxmi since the day Laxmi had arrived, a new bride, in the house—came visiting. She had visited on the second day after Laxmi's accident, and had then had to go out of town for a week to bless a newborn grandchild. Now, having returned to Delhi, she came to see. And, having seen, she said to Laxmi's sister-in-law, Ma's dadi, 'Her life is caught in her jewels. Get her sandook and put it on her chest.'

They had stared at the old woman, wondering at this seeming black magic she suggested. Surely mad, thought some. Mahendra Dada shook his head, no. There was something wrong about even trying it, he whispered to his eldest son. As if doing it would prove that they still lived in the Dark Ages. Superstitious, believing in rubbish like this.

'Do it,' said the old woman, as she left. 'Otherwise by the end of the week, you'll be left with a rotting corpse. Or not-corpse. I don't know. She's alive, but she's dead. Or the other way round. If you people have ever loved Laxmi, help her. Help her leave the world. She cannot go on her own. She needs help.'

After she had gone, they sat in silence and stared. At each other, at the dying woman, at the ants. For an hour, two hours. Then Ma's dadi rose and without asking anybody, opened the drawer of the bedside table and took out the keys to Laxmi's cupboard. She opened the cupboard, reached in, took out the large sandook. Old by now, its carved lotuses gone smooth with age, its wood darkened to a mellow café au lait. The fragrance of its sandalwood faint.

They had all been hesitating, agreeing silently that this should not be done, but when my great-grandmother brought the sandook to Laxmi's bed, nobody stopped her. Nobody said a word or lifted a finger. They waited, watched, stood aside as she bent over carefully—the sandook was heavy—and placed it on Laxmi's sunken chest.

'You'll tell me she died,' I said. I could feel a prickle at my nape. 'Or that she suddenly opened her eyes and sat up.'

Ma shook her head. 'No, she didn't get up. She took a huge, shuddering breath and let it out. Like a sigh of relief. And that was it. She was dead.'

Laxmi had never made any plans about which piece of her jewellery would go to whom. Perhaps she had refused to admit that she too was human, that she would die and would not be able to take her jewels with her, either into the pyre or into her next life. Nobody knew what to do with her sandook after she died. They did not even lift it off her chest for the next five hours, because there was this unreasonable fear in all of them...

When she had been cremated and all the rituals—four days later, thirteen days later—completed, when a month had passed and the household had settled back into its regular life, Laxmi's sister-in-law spoke to Mahendra Dada. With his permission, she opened the sandook and distributed the jewellery. All of it was shared out between Laxmi's three daughters-in-law. Mahendra Dada insisted, though, that Ma, her mother, and her grandmother take at least one large ornament each for themselves. 'I know she loved the three of you very much,' he said, 'and she would have liked—perhaps more than the bahus—for you three to have her jewels.'

And that was how Ma ended up with one of the bracelets. The other had been given to the youngest bahu.

'I refused at first,' Ma said. 'I knew I would never be able to bring myself to wear it. But Mahendra Dada was so sweet, and he so wanted me to have it. I had to give in.

'You can wear it for your drama,' Ma said, as she rose from her chair. 'It'll actually probably look quite fitting. Rich and opulent enough.'

But I did not wear it. I could not. Would not.

The Sari Satyagraha

THE WASHERWOMAN, HER sari clinging to her wet ankles as she drew water from the well, was the first to inform Sulakshana of the news. Sulakshana had been sitting on the charpai under the neem tree that grew in a corner of the courtyard. It was her favourite place, the place she always retired to after she had done the little bit of supervision that was required to keep the household moving in its well-oiled way. The masalas, the rice and the pulses had been carefully measured out and handed over to the maharaj; the vegetables had been purchased, and the gardener taken to task for not having trimmed the hedges, which were getting straggly. The local bhishti, his waterskin taut and cool, had come by to ask for the one anna due to him—and Sulakshana had, with characteristic kindness, told him to sit and have a cup of tea while he waited for the munim to bring the money.

It was, thought Sulakshana, rather silly that she should be forbidden to pay the bhishti out of the household money. 'It's a matter of principle,' her husband Vibhushan Lal Chaturvedi said. 'The bhishti doesn't bring water for the house; he brings it for the shop. So he should be paid out of the shop's accounts, not your household money. You have to be organized.'

Vibhushan Lal Chaturvedi, despite the fact that he was a mere two years older than his twenty-year-old bride, had few qualms about correcting her. His superior education and his wider experience of the world, such as it was, made him (at least in his own eyes) a being far superior to his submissive wife. He had decided opinions about everything from religion to ancient mathematics to politics, and he was not by any means shy about expressing his opinions. His acquaintances, relatives, friends and neighbours were treated, willy-nilly, to long monologues.

They were told that Hinduism preached a doubtful theology and could be much enriched by borrowing from Buddhism, Theosophy and the Brahmo Samaj. They were informed that the only sure cure for a cough was a mixture of ginger, honey and peppercorns; that painting could never be replaced by photography; and that the Treaty of Versailles had been unduly harsh on Germany. Vibhushan Lal Chaturvedi waxed eloquent on the many ills of venturing out without first drinking a glass of milk boiled with turmeric; he praised Dadasaheb Phalke's *Raja Harishchandra* to the skies; and he insisted that there was no monument in India as exquisite as the Zeenat-ul-Masajid in Delhi.

He propounded theories that seemed either utterly ancient or completely avant garde to a society that never quite knew what to expect of him.

Sulakshana bore, in large part, the brunt of her husband's admonitions and advice. 'You should not let Birju cook the spinach in mustard oil,' he would say. 'It is certain to cause flatulence.' Or, while inspecting a pile of neatly folded clothes brought in by the washerwoman: 'Surely you will not accept this? She has been beating the clothes—see, these threads are fraying.' Or, when he came home early one day and found Sulakshana sitting by herself and reading Devaki Nandan Khatri's *Chandrakanta*: 'Must you be filling your mind with such trash? If you cannot find a more uplifting book to read, tell me. I'll get some for you.' And the very next day, Sulakshana had been brought half a dozen books from the local library. They ranged from Premchand and Bhartendu Harishchandra—which Sulakshana enjoyed—to translations of Goethe and Darwin, which put her to sleep.

The young woman bore the restrictions on her reading and her management of the household stoically enough. What irked her, however, was her husband's never-ending counsel on her dress and deportment. 'I do not see why you should be wearing such an expensive sari at home, Sulakshana,' he remarked one day. He had just returned from the shop and was sitting in the courtyard sipping a cup of tea. Sulakshana was sitting before him, waving a palm-leaf fan to keep him cool.

'It's hardly expensive,' Sulakshana murmured in a moment of defiance. 'It is cotton, after all.'

Vibhushan Lal Chaturvedi put down his cup and stared at his wife, horror writ all over his thin clean-shaven face. 'It is a jamdani,' he said. 'A Dhaka muslin. It may be cotton, but it is expensive. You cannot hope to fool me.'

Sulakshana, flushed with annoyance, looked down at the offending sari. It was a beautiful piece of work, a phulwar, with floral motifs woven into an elegant blue-black ground. It had been a gift from an old aunt, and Sulakshana knew well enough that her husband probably knew—to the nearest anna—how much it cost. He, after all, did not own a sari shop for nothing.

She did not say anything, and her husband picked up

his cup again. 'From now on, let me not find you wearing expensive clothes at home,' he said. 'You of all people should know how things are. The poverty, the oppression, the turmoil in this country—the mind boggles.' He shook his head unhappily. 'The Great War has not been over two years, and here you are, behaving in this extravagant fashion. Next we know, you'll be dressing up in a Banarasi to go to the temple.'

The arrival of a chance visitor had put an end to the conversation but from that day on, Sulakshana was allowed to only wear dull cotton saris at home. If she had to go out, she was permitted to drape herself in something slightly expensive, such as a jamdani. Her richly embroidered kanthas, her jamawars and paithanis and tanchois, were put by and unearthed only at Diwali, or on the rare occasion of a wedding.

That day, Sulakshana was wearing a rather battered old tangail, an off-white sari woven with a pretty border of black and red. It had seen better days—the hem was frayed, and there were a few spots of turmeric that even good strong sunlight had not been able to banish. Sulakshana was sitting cross-legged on the charpai, a well-polished brass paandaan cradled in her lap. She was busy cracking the supari when the washerwoman squatted down near her for a chat, squeezing the water out of the end of her sari as she did so.

'There was quite a commotion at the ghat this morning,' the washerwoman said, apropos of nothing. She loved a bit of gossip, and Sulakshana, who had nothing better to do, had no objections to hearing it. She put aside the supari cracker and wiped her hands on her sari.

'Why? What had happened?'

'Some students from the English College had gathered at the ghat and were shouting slogans against the British. The police came and arrested all of them, each and every one. And you know, bibiji, those students didn't utter a squeak about being dragged off to the police station. That was what really surprised me, the way they happily let themselves be taken away—'

Sulakshana was more in the know than the washerwoman. 'Ah,' she said, going back to her task, 'That's because of the Non-Cooperation Movement, Lajwanti. Gandhiji has called for everybody to boycott the British, you know. He has said people should not touch anything that is even vaguely British. So students should leave schools and colleges that are sponsored by the British, government servants should leave their jobs, people should not use public transport. Things like that.'

Lajwanti looked at Sulakshana in wonder, as if Sulakshana herself were exhorting her to all these heroic— and unusual—feats of protest.

'The country will come to a standstill, bibiji,' she said, in an awed voice. 'How will we manage?'

'The way we managed before the British arrived,' replied her mistress, with a faint smile.

'But where is the sense in deliberately getting arrested? The students could have easily escaped, bibiji, but I saw them letting themselves be arrested. That's sheer stupidity— why would anybody want to do that?'

Sulakshana shrugged. 'I have no idea,' she said quietly. 'But Gandhiji has said that it will help the Freedom Movement, so I suppose he must be right.'

Lajwanti had to be satisfied with this answer but Sulakshana herself came to know much more about the Non-

Cooperation Movement, civil disobedience, satyagraha, and non-violent resistance that very evening. Her husband, who had also heard news of the arrests, took it upon himself to educate her.

'Gandhiji used satyagraha as a successful way to protest when he was in South Africa,' he told her as they sat on the veranda after dinner. Sulakshana was mending a tear in one of her saris, and Vibhushan Lal Chaturvedi was chewing a paan and gazing pensively out onto the moonlit garden.

'And not just in South Africa, but also in Champaran and Kheda. Everywhere, even the poorest of people have come together in an organized way to protest—peacefully, mind you—against oppression. It has worked in the past, it should work now. Gandhiji has a lot of foresight, Sulakshana. You mark my words—if there is one man who can win freedom for this country, it is he. He alone can show us the way.'

Sulakshana did not say anything. She did not need to; her husband was quite happy listening to his own voice.

'There are other leaders who're very sceptical, of course—Bal Gangadhar Tilak and Jinnah, plus some others, including Annie Besant—but that is to be expected. You can't hope to please everybody. What matters is that the younger generation are all for it. The Congress is supporting it completely, and already hundreds of people are leaving cushy jobs with the government in order to enlist with the Congress.'

He droned on, recounting to a bored Sulakshana all the events of the past few weeks that seemed to indicate the increasing antagonism of the people to British rule. He extolled the right-mindedness of leaders like Maulana Azad and Mukhtar Ahmed Ansari, who supported the

Non-Cooperation Movement. He rattled off, as if he had learnt them all by rote (and Sulakshana wondered privately if he had actually done so), all the major incidents of civil disobedience in the past week. Sulakshana was told, in painstaking and tedious detail, of each arrest in the city; of each case of refusing to salute the Union Jack; of each episode that smacked even faintly of resistance to British rule. She was yawning surreptitiously by the time her husband finally sat back in his chair and said, 'It's time we were asleep. Don't want to be late getting up tomorrow morning, do we?'

Sulakshana's interactions with the outside world were limited to the small-time traders and hawkers who came by with their wares, the servants and a small circle of friends and relatives whom she occasionally visited, along with her husband. From these people, and from the newspapers that her husband insisted she read—'For heavens' sake, you're not illiterate! Use your education, Sulakshana. Read, read!'—she managed to remain somewhat abreast of what was happening. But it was, ultimately, her husband who directed her.

About a week after the mass arrest at the ghat, Vibhushan Lal Chaturvedi came home to announce to his wife that their household was going to be joining the Non-Cooperation Movement.

Sulakshana, who was sitting on the bed and sewing buttons on to her husband's kurta, looked up in surprise. 'Joining the movement?' she said faintly. 'But why? I mean—how? As it is, we do nothing to support the British.'

Her husband took off his neat black achkan and hung it up before turning back to her. 'You may not think so, Sulakshana,' he explained patiently. 'But unwittingly, we—and I don't mean just the two of us, but also the servants—may be doing a lot of things that help support this colonial government. It's wrong, absolutely and utterly and completely wrong. We're killing our own motherland, Sulakshana. Have you no patriotism in you?'

Sulakshana did not respond to this melodramatic piece of rhetoric, and her husband continued. 'For instance. When you go to the market or to visit your old school friend, you use public transport. Now that is support of the British government.'

'But I go in Manohar's ikka,' said Sulakshana plaintively, a protest that drew a scowl from her husband.

'But do the servants do the same? No, they don't—'

'They walk,' Sulakshana interrupted gently.

'All right, all right—maybe not as far as public transport goes, but there are other ways. We should stop using anything that is manufactured abroad. Be Indian, buy Indian. So no more of these fancy things you keep filling the house with. We are not here to help support the British economy. We have to look to our interests first, the interests of our nation—'

Sulakshana cut in again, this time not quite so gently. 'Your hair oil is English,' she pointed out. 'And your shoes. And the tailor who made those smart jackets of yours was also British, I think.'

'Certainly not! He was not British, he was a Goan gentleman. Part Portuguese, maybe, but very definitely not British. You cannot expect me to burn up my jackets just because the man who made them is Goan. That would be silly. But yes, the hair oil must be thrown out. Get Birju to buy me some coconut oil when he goes to the market tomorrow.'

He paused a while, chewing thoughtfully at his upper lip. 'There is so much that can be done,' he said. 'So much. We must do our bit, Sulakshana. It would be a shame if we didn't.'

His wife nodded, and for a change (considering her recent volubility) did not say anything. Vibhushan Lal Chaturvedi frowned to himself, and then, unable to think of anything else to say, went off to the room he liked to call his study.

Her husband may not have said anything further on the topic, but Sulakshana's sister-in-law, who came visiting the next morning, had much to say. Devaki was a stout, richly dressed woman with a deceptively jovial exterior that hid an iron will. She was a good twelve years older than her brother, and was one of the very few people who paid no heed whatsoever to Vibhushan Lal Chaturvedi's many strictures. Fortunately for Sulakshana, this formidable lady had developed, almost from the day Sulakshana was married, a soft corner for her brother's timid young bride.

Devaki bustled into the house shortly after ten in the morning, accompanied by two children and a servant carrying a large basket of mangoes. The servant was sent off towards the kitchen, the children were handed into the care of a maid with clear instructions not to let them wander near the well and the lady herself turned to Sulakshana.

'Come along, child,' Devaki commanded, her bangles jangling as she caught Sulakshana's arm and steered her towards the charpai under the neem tree. 'I have something to say to you—here, Birju'—she broke off to yell—'some tea, and bring the sugar separately!'

The charpai creaked as Devaki lowered herself on to it. Sulakshana sat down, her hand automatically picking up the palm leaf fan. Devaki talked of this and that—her children, her husband, an excellent recipe for lime pickle—until Birju brought the tea. When he had returned to the kitchen and the two women were alone, she said, 'What have you done to yourself?'

Sulakshana reddened, but she did not look at Devaki. She stared down into the milky brown depths of the cup she was holding, and said, 'I don't know what you mean. I am perfectly well, didi.'

'You are well, I can see that,' Devaki snapped. 'I am not commenting about your health. And well you know it!' She put her cup down and reached across to caress Sulakshana's head in a distinctly maternal way. 'Why are you looking so neglected, child? Is that fool to blame for this?'

Sulakshana shook her head vigorously. 'There is nothing wrong with me, didi,' she persisted. 'Nothing at all.'

'Then why, pray, are you dressed like a beggar woman?' retorted Devaki acidly. 'Vibhushan Lal Chaturvedi's wife, a rich young lady if I ever saw one, wearing little better than rags!'

Sulakshana bit her lip unhappily.

'Well?'

'It—it's not good to be wearing expensive saris at home,' she whimpered.

'Hah! Parroting what that dolt of a husband of yours has told you, if I'm not mistaken.' Devaki's eyes glittered. 'Is that it? Did he tell you to stop wearing decent clothes at home?'

'He said it would not do for me to be extravagant. The war is barely over, and people are poor and oppressed...' her voice trailed off, betraying a serious lack of conviction.

Devaki tut-tutted. 'And you listened to him. Pray how

will your wearing rags help the poor and oppressed?' She waited for an answer, but since Sulakshana did not oblige her with one, she continued. 'He may be my brother, Sulakshana, but I am under no delusions. He is a fool, and you're a greater fool if you let him dictate such things to you. Let him concern himself with trade and politics and other such matters. Where the household is concerned— and most importantly, where you are concerned—he cannot tell you what you should do and what you shouldn't. You're the woman of the house, child. Show a little spirit!'

She sipped noisily from the cup of tea and then added, somewhat as an afterthought, 'And if I see you wearing those tatters the next time I come, I will personally dress you up in something more suitable.'

The conversation wandered on to other topics, and Devaki did not touch upon Sulakshana's sartorial inadequacies any more. By the time she finally left—which was after a long and leisurely lunch—she seemed to have forgotten all about it. She hugged Sulakshana briefly, assured her that a jar of lime pickle would be sent the following day, and extended an invitation to dinner whenever Sulakshana and her husband should find it convenient.

Sulakshana stood at the gate for a few minutes after the ikka had disappeared in a cloud of dust down the lane. She looked lost in thought, and when she eventually turned and went back into the house, she had much on her mind.

Vibhushan Lal Chaturvedi entered his house that evening to find his wife draped in a gossamer-light Chanderi sari. It was a delicate apple green in colour, with a thin border and butis of deep red, embellished with gold thread. It had been, if his memory served him right, gifted to Sulakshana by Devaki. Bought at his own shop, too. An expensive sari— and she was wearing it at home.

Vibhushan Lal Chaturvedi stood at the door of the room and gaped. 'You—you're wearing a Chanderi,' he gasped unnecessarily.

Sulakshana turned to him and smiled blithely. 'Yes. Devaki didi had given it to me, don't you remember?'

'Yes—yes, of course I remember,' he replied, halfway between angry and astonished at this unexpected rebellion.

Devaki put down the vase in which she had been arranging flowers and, with a look of quiet joy on her face, glanced down at the billowing pleats of the sari. 'Isn't it beautiful?'

'And expensive,' her husband snapped. 'I think I told you not to wear your good saris at home.'

'Of course,' Sulakshana replied, looking up at him with limpid eyes. 'But you told me that I should do my bit for the Freedom Movement, you know.'

Her husband stared at her in consternation. 'What does the Freedom Movement have to do with your saris?'

'Lajwanti told me yesterday that they're also burning cloth. Cotton cloth. There was a huge bonfire near the vegetable market, so I took Lajwanti along, and gave away all my cotton saris. Gandhiji would approve, wouldn't he?'

Vibhushan Lal Chaturvedi sank back against the richly carved teak cupboard behind him. Perspiration had broken out on his forehead, and for almost a minute, he felt as if the room was whirling around him in a mad, gleeful dance of malice. He closed his eyes and swallowed hard, trying desperately to control the rising panic.

When he opened his eyes, Sulakshana was looking at him anxiously.

'You burnt your saris,' her husband croaked. 'But your saris were Indian, completely and absolutely Indian. They're only burning British cloth. Why did you burn your saris?'

Her face fell. 'I didn't know that,' she said. 'I thought all cotton clothes had to be burnt. I'm sorry—but I haven't given any of your clothes, I didn't know if you'd want that. So that's all right, isn't it?' she added brightly. And her husband, for once at a loss for words, could do nothing but nod.

Sulakshana smiled to herself as she went off towards the kitchen. Devaki didi would approve of her improved wardrobe.

And Lajwanti, much enriched by the windfall of a dozen cotton saris, would not think herself too poor any more.

Wronged

'DIDN'T YOU SLEEP on the flight? Look at the bags under your eyes.'

'Get lost, you. And hey, watch that suitcase—I don't want it getting—ahh! There—I knew you'd do something of the sort! Manish told me I should take the old one—here, give it to me. Just look what you've gone and done.'

Vicky watched, arms folded across his chest, as his sister heaved the huge crimson suitcase into the back of his SX4. 'You moron,' Meera grumbled as she straightened up, her fingers rubbing vigorously at a long scar across the side of the bag. 'Do you know how much that cost?'

'And you do know that *I* know that scratch has been there for the past three years? Come on, get in. Let's go home.'

Meera looked up at him, her eyes her most visible feature, what with that heavy black eyeliner she insisted on wearing so thick. Sharmila Tagore style, Vicky used to tease her. All that was needed was a beehive-like bouffant and an itsy-bitsy blue swimsuit, and she'd be ready to face the camera. She was still lovely, but in a more mature way.

'How's Manish?' Vicky asked, shutting the boot. 'I thought he'd come, too.'

'Good God, why? To see the family's dirty linen being washed?'

They separated, Vicky going to the driver's side, Meera to the passenger's. Vicky spoke up only when he had started the car, tugged his seat belt on, and adjusted the rear-view mirror.

'You mean you haven't told him?'

She reached up to scrunch her shoulder-length hair, grey in strands and a little straggly at the ends, into an untidy bun that she secured with a black plastic clip. 'Of course I've told him. I just didn't think it necessary to have him along. He has to look after the children, too, no? Nikhil has his exams coming up, and Neena has to be taken for her dance classes, and—' she sighed. 'Oh, hell. What's the point? I didn't bring him because it would be so embarrassing. *I* am embarrassed. Vicky, how did this happen?'

Vicky shrugged. 'I don't know. Belt up. This is Delhi, not your beloved Pune. I'll get a challan if you aren't wearing your seat belt.'

'Bullshit.' But she pulled the belt across her chest and down, and clipped it in anyway. The car was moving forward, out past the row of waiting radio taxis and private cars.

'I need coffee,' Meera said. 'I'm so bloody exhausted.' She squeezed her eyes shut and laid the back of her hand across her eyelids, her elbow resting on the glass of the window beside her. 'Haven't slept a wink ever since I got to know—oh, God. Oh, God, oh God oh God. *How?*' A tear, escaping under an eyelid, ran down her cheek, and she swiped at it.

'The nearest is Vasant Vihar,' Vicky said, pretending not to notice. 'There's a Costa Coffee there, and a Barista. You can take your pick.'

* * *

'A public place perhaps wasn't such a good idea, after all,' Meera mumbled. She was hunched over a cappuccino—grande, with an extra shot of espresso—and had a rumpled paper napkin, soggy with tears, clutched in one fist. 'Now I've gone and made a fool of myself. Why didn't you get me out of here when you saw how crowded it was?'

'How was I to know you'd burst into tears all over again? After you went off to sleep in the car, I thought you'd be all right. Drink up, now. Nobody's looking, anyway.'

'Ya. Because I'm not crying any more.' She made a face. 'Am I looking like a raccoon? Has my eyeliner run?'

'I don't know. I can't tell.' He took a bite from his croissant.

A crack of laughter burst from the table at the window overlooking the pavement. Two tables, actually, because they had been joined together to accommodate the group. A motley group, ranging in age from perhaps six to sixty. Men, women, children. Old, young, in between. That sudden laughter, overheard even above the piped music, set off a chain of giggles and guffaws. Meera glared at them over her shoulder, before turning back to stare into her mug.

'We used to be like that,' she said. 'Till six months back. Family.'

'We still are family. Don't be so melodramatic.'

'Melodramatic? I'm being melo—'

'Shh! Please.' Vicky leaned over, placed a hand on her wrist. She snatched her arm away. But when she spoke, her voice was lower, quieter. More controlled, even if the anger was merely suppressed, not dissipated. 'You think you have any bloody right to tell me to stop being what I am? You?

You, staying right here in Delhi, and you didn't know what was happening?'

'How could I have known what was happening? I don't stay with them any more, remember? We're not even in the same fucking state—'

'*Technically* speaking. How far apart are Gurgaon and Delhi? Huh? You come to GK or Khan Market every other day to meet your friends and business acquaintants. And it's not as if you haven't been visiting'—she swallowed—'them.'

'Mummy and Papa,' Vicky said, in a stifled voice. 'Not *them*. Mummy and Papa.' He tore off a bit of the croissant and dunked it in his coffee. 'And no, I don't meet them that often. Once a month, or so. I don't keep tabs on them, for God's sake.'

Conversation ebbed and flowed about them. A waiter came by with a tray to clear a nearby table. The smell of coffee hung in the air, warm and comforting. The family at the two tables had gone quiet, now busy with sandwiches, huge wedges of carrot cake, muffins. Cold coffees. 'The last time I was in Delhi,' Meera said in a bitter little voice, 'all of us had gone out. Do you remember? To that restaurant in Khan Market. To celebrate forty years of their being married. *Forty* years. Papa had looked so proud. Mummy had worn that blue Banarasi sari.' She paused, blinking away a tear, turning to look unseeingly out of the window. 'Look at me,' she said, with a forced grin, 'crying at the drop of a hat.'

She took a deep breath, then picked up her cappuccino and sipped at it. 'Who would have thought it, huh? I was looking at the photos we took back then. Less than a year ago. How Mummy has her head snuggled against Papa's neck in one picture. His arm around her shoulders. The smiles. Who would have thought she was all the time having an affair with someone else?'

* * *

'What did Papa tell you?' She asked, as she slid into the passenger seat and reached for the seat belt.

'What did he tell *you*?'

'Nothing. Why do you think I'm asking you? Turn up the AC, Vicky. It's so bloody hot in here.' Meera pressed the button to slide the window down, and pulled out a pair of sunglasses from the bag on her lap. She put them on now and stared at the wall four feet away, half-covered with cascades of magenta bougainvillea.

'I called after you rang off, you know,' she said. 'Mummy picked up, but I couldn't bring myself to say anything to her. And Papa—well. He said everything was all right. Nothing was wrong. Nothing.'

The car slid gently out of the parking slot, away from the bougainvillea and the wall. Meera put the window back up, but did not turn to look at her younger brother. 'Tell me, Vicky,' she said when they were out of Vasant Vihar and on the Outer Ring Road. 'Tell me how you found out.'

He did not answer immediately. A passing scooterist swerved sharply across in front of the car to avoid a pair of fighting mongrels, and Vicky screeched to a halt. 'These—' he began to say, and left the sentence hanging in the air. 'Damn this traffic,' he muttered. 'It gets worse every day.'

'Vicky.'

'Yes, yes.' He sounded irritated, and flustered. And he looked older—a good dozen years older—than his twenty-eight. He was bleary-eyed and had developed, over the past three years or so, a definite paunch. Right now, the unshaven jaw, the crumpled T-shirt, and the jeans that should have been washed at least a week ago added to the look of self-neglect.

'I had to go to Nehru Place to meet a client,' he said. 'I had estimated a meeting of at least an hour, but just as I was nearing CR Park, he phoned. To say someone had died, and he had to cancel the meeting. I was *so* close.' He changed gears, speeding up to pass a garbage-laden truck that was trundling slowly along, leaving a trail of polythene bags, rotting vegetable peels, and a stench that made its way into the car.

'Phew. What was I saying? Yeah—that day when my client ditched me. So I could turn right around and return to Gurgaon. Three hours' drive for nothing. Or I could see if any friends were free for coffee—no, don't bite my head off, I'm getting around to it. Basically, I decided to be a good son and pop in all unannounced.'

'And?'

'And when I got there, Papa was out. I saw that immediately, the car was gone. But the gate wasn't locked, so I knew Mummy must be home.' Ahead of them, the digital display below a traffic light blinked down to zero, and a bright yellow Nano crashed the light, narrowly missing the sudden deluge of buses and autos and cars coming from the left. A flurry of angry honking followed the Nano.

'I was parking in the shade of that gulmohar tree opposite their house when I saw a car draw up outside. An ordinary car, nothing fancy. Old, slightly battered. It didn't honk, or anything, but I saw Mummy come out, down the driveway, to open the gate. I saw the car go in. She walked in, shut the gate behind her. I saw the car door open. It was a man. I couldn't see him at that distance, but I'm quite sure it was nobody I knew.'

'Did he stay inside long?'

'An hour. At first, I thought it was probably somebody she'd been expecting for some work—you know, bank work, insurance, things like that. These guys come home to do all the paperwork for you.' He gave her a sheepish look in exchange for the derisive one she had cast his way. 'Yes, I know. It sounds dumb, now that I think of it.'

'She wouldn't come out to open the gate for him if it was just one of those guys,' Meera said scornfully. 'In any case, Mummy never does any of that for herself—Papa's always handled all the paperwork for her investments, her insurance. Everything.' She reached out, adjusted the louvres of the air-conditioning duct, and murmured, 'You were trying to give her a chance, weren't you? You were hoping it wasn't what you suspected.'

Vicky said nothing.

'Then? He came out after an hour?'

'No. I went in. I—I couldn't bear it any more.'

The light turned green. Almost instantly, a cacophony broke out. Angry honking, a car in the front accelerating and racing away, a motorcyclist banging on the side of an auto that had stalled and was blocking his path. Vicky slipped into the middle lane and kept going.

'For Christ's sake—can't you get a move on?' Meera burst out. 'Don't give me these dramatic pauses. You're not a bloody storyteller, and I don't have the strength left to keep asking you what happened next!'

He gave her a terse nod. 'I rang the doorbell. I kept

on ringing, twice, thrice. Then I phoned her to say it was me, and was she out? She said yes, she was. Gone to the market.' He slowed down to let a woman with a toddler climb onto the pavement. 'So I asked her which market. Said I was in the vicinity, so I wanted to meet up, and could I come home? Or come and pick her up and give her a lift home?'

Meera's knuckles, clutching at the handles of her bag, had gone white.

'She said she was meeting up with friends for lunch. They would pick her up from the market in five minutes' time. She said she was sorry to have missed me.'

'Oh, *God*.'

'Hmm. I said it was all right, then. I'd see her some other time. How was Papa. Stuff like that. Then I came back to the car, got in and drove round the corner and waited. If she was looking out—she must have been, I guess—she'd know I'd gone.' Vicky swallowed. 'Look, Meera, I don't like saying all this. It's horrible. To sneak like this about my own mother. I felt sick then, but it was more curiosity than anything else—I just couldn't bring myself to believe it could be anything. Anything *wrong*. Mummy? I mean, Mummy has always been so perfect. Such a good mother. Such a good wife.'

'How do you know how good a wife she's been? Have you had to live with her as a husband? Have you asked Papa?' Meera gave him a look of withering scorn, and Vicky flushed.

'Go on,' she said, after a while. 'We're nearing, aren't we? If you don't hurry up, we'll get there, and I won't even have heard it all.'

'We can always stop at the market up ahead. There's a Café Coffee Day there.'

'More coffee? I shouldn't—oh, what the hell. You don't realize you have an adulteress for a mother every day.'

She did not have coffee after all. Just a lemonade, with extra ice. A tall glass of it. 'And get me something to eat, Vicky.'

'Brownies? That's the only thing they've got. Or samosas.'

'A brownie. With chocolate sauce. Do they have vanilla ice cream too? Two scoops.'

Vicky looked at her with a raised eyebrow, but only nodded.

'I walked back and watched from behind a tree,' Vicky said when they had settled down again. This coffee shop was quieter than the last one had been, quieter and less crowded. At the far end, a small group of high school students, still in their school uniforms, were laughing and chatting over what looked like never-ending glasses of frappe. Here and there were scattered lone laptop users, gazing into screens and occasionally sipping from half-forgotten cups.

'He came out soon after. Mummy saw him out and then, when he'd got into the car and gone, she closed the gate and went in.' He looked up, murmured a quick thank you to the waiter who placed his coffee, her lemonade and the brownie on the table. Waited till the man had gone, and then turned back to Meera. 'There's not much more, actually. I tried to follow the man, but I lost him. Traffic is so horrible, you know—and his car was so nondescript.'

He sipped his coffee, and without asking, dipped his teaspoon into the vanilla ice cream on Meera's plate. 'But I took a few days' leave from my office, and started keeping a watch on the house. Do you know, every day—as soon as

Papa's gone for his golf, or to the club, or wherever—that man turns up? It cannot be a coincidence, can it? Papa out, man in.' He cringed. 'Oh, shit. That sounded foul.'

Meera did not react. She was using her fork to trace patterns in the pool of chocolate sauce on her plate. One set of furrows swirling about, like a wave. Another, straight and harsh as the bars of a prison cell. 'Papa isn't home much, is he?' she remarked, her voice soft. 'He has so much to do, doesn't he?'

Vicky shrugged. 'He always was a busy man. Don't you remember, when we were kids? Or, rather, you were in college, and I was a kid'—the nod to the ten years' difference in their ages—'how rarely we'd be up when he came home?'

'I used to be, sometimes,' Meera said. 'If I stayed up really late, reading or watching TV.' She cut into her brownie, speared it on the tines of the fork, and rubbed it in the chocolate sauce. 'Mummy used to sit up for him, even if he came near midnight. She would've eaten her dinner, of course, but she would sit beside him and talk. I used to overhear their conversations, sometimes. She'd ask him what he'd done all day long, what had happened at work. She'd tell him what had happened at school, or when she got home. About us. About—well, everything other than Papa and his office. Can I have that teaspoon? I don't know why they haven't given me a spoon. Do they expect me to eat the ice cream with a bloody fork? Idiots.'

She scooped up the ice cream with the borrowed teaspoon, shovelling the brownie and sauce onto it. 'Mmm. Want some?'

Vicky shook his head. 'You've got a chocolate moustache. What were you saying?'

Meera fiddled with the spoon, dipping it in the chocolate, licking the back of it. 'I don't know,' she said, quietly. 'If it were someone else—not Mummy, not Papa—perhaps I could have been more objective. But they are my parents, all said and done. People I've known all my life. I thought I knew them.' She looked up, her eyes full of pain. 'I cannot come to terms with this. With'—she swallowed—'Mummy having an *affair*? You don't think of your parents as having sex lives.'

Vicky flushed. '*Meera.*'

'Yes, I know. I know. I was just saying. *Good* Indian parents like ours kept their affection for each other under wraps, no? Did you ever see them even kiss each other on the cheek? Did you ever hear any sounds from their bedroom, other than Papa's snores? Or Mummy reminding him about some family function we had to attend?'

Vicky gestured, his fingers fluttering, as if trying to negate what she said, waving away her words.

'It's true, Vicky. You know that. We never think that way in this country, do we? Everything is so prim and proper. It's others who do things like that. Others who sleep around. Do you sleep around, Vicky?' She gave him a sly smile, but it was also a sad smile. 'Not that you're even married yet, so it shouldn't matter.'

'Shut up,' he hissed. 'Just shut up, Meera. What I do or don't isn't the question here. What do we do?' He took up his mug and drank down half of it in one great gulp. 'Papa must feel so awful. So humiliated. *Wronged.*'

There was a sudden burst of muzak, the usually soft instrumentals played at low volume inexplicably belted out high enough to be strident, piercing. There was a collective wincing. Someone yelled in anger, and there was a flurry as one of the baristas sprinted to the end of the counter. The music sank again into the depths. A low, soothing murmur. Quiet, gentle, going its own unobtrusive way.

'You told Papa,' Meera said. 'What did you say? Was Mummy there?'

Vicky shook his head. 'I did not have the nerve to say it when she was around. I phoned Papa one day and asked him if he'd have lunch with me. He was at the club, as usual. With his golf buddies. He didn't like giving up his time with them, but he agreed.' He stirred what remained of his coffee, digging up the bitter dregs. 'I told him what I had seen. That was all.'

'And? What was his reaction?'

'He said I should mind my own business. That it didn't concern me.'

Conversation ebbed and flowed about them. Words, uttered but unheard here in their little corner. Chair legs scraping on the floor as someone got up. The sound of crockery, the burble and splutter of the coffee machine. The music, now back on an even keel.

'Did you go back?' Meera asked, her tone neutral. 'Did you push Papa? Talk to Mummy?'

Vicky shook his head. 'I didn't have the nerve to. Papa clammed up at that lunch, he changed the conversation, you know, after that. Began talking politics and the stock market. Even when I went to see him off to his car, he gave me a look—you know how scary he can be. And Mummy? I'm too embarrassed. I wouldn't know where to start. That's why I phoned you.'

'Do they know I'm coming?'

'Mummy does. She answered the phone when I called her last evening. Papa had gone out to Mr Sridhar's place for bridge. She must have told him, I suppose.'

Meera scraped the remains of the brownie from her plate and licked the spoon clean. 'Well, then. If it has to be done, it has to be done. I think it would be best if I offered to take them to Pune, what do you think? I talked to Manish, and he said that would be good—get Mummy away—' she stopped. 'What happened? Why're you frowning like that?'

'You shouldn't have told Manish everything.' Vicky's voice was a low grumble.

'Why not? He's my husband, and he's my best friend. I told you, didn't I, that I told him? What reason should I have given for coming away to Delhi so suddenly?' She sighed. 'Forget it. You won't understand. Ask for the bill. Let's go.'

* * *

Meera leaned her elbow on the railing of the balcony, her chin resting in her cupped hand. Vicky sat opposite her, slumped in an old cane chair, its block-printed red and green cushions faded and squashed.

'What is she doing?' Vicky asked.

Meera looked down at the lone figure, sitting on the wooden bench under the gulmohar tree that grew in one corner of the garden but spread its canopy, with its withered flame-red flowers, across all the lawn. 'Nothing. Just sitting there, with her hands in her lap.'

'Is'—Vicky hesitated, his voice shook—'is Mummy crying?'

'I can't tell. She's too far away. I don't think so.'

The high-pitched squeaks of a squirrel sounded from the gulmohar. The woman on the bench did not look up, did not stir.

'What did you say to her? Did you tell her about taking them away to Pune with you?'

Meera looked up at the blue sky above, at the fluffy white clouds near the far horizon. 'I never got around to it,' she said, her voice barely audible. 'We talked of other things.'

'What do you mean? Do you mean you never asked her—'

'Let us go, Vicky,' Meera said, looking him straight in the eye. Her own eyes were brimming with tears. 'I'll come back later to say goodbye, but let's just slip out for now, okay? Please?'

He stared at her, puzzled. 'Where do you want to go? What's wrong?'

But Meera had already risen to her feet, had picked up her handbag and slung it over her shoulder. She slipped a hand under his elbow and tugged. 'Please. Let's just go. I need to go away from this house. Even if it's only for an hour. We'll go to a park, a garden. Any place where it's quiet, peaceful.'

'You're worrying me,' Vicky said when they had sat down on a metal bench, its paint peeling, in the park opposite the house. A venerable old maulsari tree, its dark green leaves glossy, spread itself above them. Below, scattered on the scrubby grass, were the little star-like white flowers, now brown and limp at the tips of the petals, from the tree. Meera had collected some of them—the freshest and most unspoilt of the lot—and was holding them in one cupped palm. Raising them to her nose, sniffing, trailing a fingertip through the blossoms.

'What happened?' Vicky asked, when she did not react. 'Tell me.'

'Word for word, everything we said? I can't, I don't remember.' She lifted out one of the maulsari blossoms, more perfect than the others, its feathery petals still crisp and white. 'We talked,' she said. 'Mummy told me about herself. I told her about me, about being married. About Manish and I.' She lifted the flower up, raising her arm high so that the last rays of the sun shone down on the flower. 'Look how pretty it is, Vicky. Isn't it? When you see it from this far, you can't see any flaws. Those little wilted ends, the bits gone brown—you don't see any of that. Just the pretty perfection.'

Vicky stared, his eyes watchful.

Meera lowered her arm. She had let the rest of the flowers slide from her palm onto the grass. This one she held still, between the tips of her thumb and forefinger. 'When you phoned me, my first thought was to hate her, you know.' She twirled the flower slowly as she spoke. 'Even later, when I had recovered enough from the shock to be able to think over it carefully, I saw it only from one point of view. Papa's. I thought how wronged he must feel. I felt so sorry for him. I couldn't *hate* Mummy, I realized that—I never can—but I still blamed her.'

Up above them, a bird started calling in the maulsari. An odd call, kot-roo, kot-roo, kot-roo. Meera squinted up, her eyes searching among the branches. 'See?' she whispered. 'A barbet. So difficult to see, so impossible to miss hearing.'

Vicky did not look up. Meera, her head still tilted up, her eyes still on the elusive barbet, said, 'How long was I with Mummy? How long did we speak?'

'Three hours. A little more.'

'It didn't seem like enough.' She bent her head, looked down at her hands, at the maulsari flower in her cupped palm. 'She did not tell me about—about that man. I didn't ask her, either. Who he is, how she met him, what. I just told her what you had seen. And I asked her if she thought it was time she and Papa moved away from here. A change, that was what I said. Something new.'

Vicky winced.

'Yah. Wrong choice of words. I thought so too, after I'd said it.' Meera paused. 'But you know something? Mummy only laughed. Not a real laugh, but still. She saw the irony in it.'

She looked up at him, and Vicky saw that there were tears in her eyes. 'Mummy has always been so lonely, Vicky. So terribly lonely. You and I never saw it, did we? Even when it was so obvious to us. She always seemed so busy, so bustling, that it never struck us that one can be a whirlpool of activity and an island at the same time. We had our own lives to lead, and the one person who had promised to spend the rest of his life with her didn't have the time for it. Still doesn't.'

'You have to give each other space in a marriage,' Vicky protested. But the words were mumbled, a half-hearted attempt to repeat something he thought he believed in.

'There's a difference between giving someone space and neglecting them. I don't expect Papa to invite Mummy to play golf with him. I don't expect him to stay at home every day, spending all his time beside her. She doesn't expect it, either. She has her books to read, the few friends she still chats with now and then. TV. Housework. What she doesn't have is the man she had thought she would grow old with. She has never had him.' She looked away, towards the setting sun. 'He has never been a spouse. Paying some of the bills and deciding which schools we would go to, or where we would go during our summer vacations—that is not all there is to being a husband.'

She sighed. 'You don't understand, do you?'

'Papa was a good father,' Vicky said stubbornly.

'But not a good husband, perhaps.' She stood up. 'Come, Vicky. Let's go. I promised Mummy I'd be back home before sunset. She must be waiting.'

* * *

The last of the relatives and friends had gone. Meera's husband, Manish, had stood beside her, nodding, talking to people, acknowledging the murmured condolences, the brief reminiscence, the quick squeeze of a hand when someone could not find words to speak. Vicky had been there, too, closer to the main entrance of the crematorium, his crumpled blue T-shirt and jeans contrasting oddly with the crisp white kurta and pajama that Papa wore.

'So composed,' an old lady, one of Papa's many cousins, had murmured as she held Meera's hand and looked towards Papa. 'So calm and collected. Poor man, what he must be going through.'

'Who would have thought,' said Vicky, as they stood on the balcony that evening, just the two of them. 'I mean, it was—what? A month back?—when you came here? That brief trip, just after we'd discovered.' He heaved a deep sigh. 'And now she's gone. Gone, just like that.'

The moon had risen. From somewhere down the lane came the strident whistle of a neighbourhood watchman on patrol. Four hours later, five, when the lights would be out in most houses, the man would probably settle down, seating himself on a folding metal chair next to the gate of the park.

'She knew,' Meera said. 'She knew, back then.'

'What?' Vicky stared, horrified. 'But—but why didn't she say anything? No, wait. How do you know? Did she tell you? Why didn't you say anything to me?'

'Shut up,' Meera replied, her voice weary. 'Of course she told me. What do you think, I've got ESP? She told me not to tell anybody. It was her only wish.'

'But why on earth? I'm sure she could have been saved—'

'She could not be saved.' Meera looked down, at her hands where they rested on the railing. 'Or she did not really want to even try, I think. I don't know.' A tear slid down her cheek, all the way to her chin. In a stray ray of light shining from the bulb at the far end of the balcony, Vicky saw the tear tremble on the tip of his sister's chin. It fell, dripping onto her hand.

'Mummy had been to a specialist,' she said. 'They could have done surgery, but they said it would only be temporary. That it was certain to come back.' She lifted a hand to wipe her cheek. 'And she had decided she did not want to go through it. She told me she had had as much of life as she could take.'

'Why didn't you try to talk to her? There's always hope! While there's even a little bit of hope, how can one just give up?' Vicky burst out. He was not crying, but Meera could hear the tears in his voice. 'Didn't you tell her how much we would miss her?'

'If you miss her so much, you could have lived here,' Meera pointed out. 'Or I could. If it was so very impossible to live without her, neither of us need ever have moved away.' She had stopped crying now. 'We had our own lives to lead, Vicky. Mummy knew that. And she did not grudge us that. She told me that she loved us, and that she knew we would miss her. But that it was useless.' She leaned her elbows on the railing and looked down at the garden, now illuminated by the evenly spaced little lights along its edge. 'She told me not to tell anyone because she did not want to have to try and explain herself.'

'What about—what about the man she…' Vicky swallowed, finding it hard to utter the words. 'The man she was having an affair with?'

Meera winced. 'Don't put it like that.'

'Why not? The truth is the truth. Saying it in pretty words isn't going to change it.'

Meera looked down at where her fingers rested on the railing, the nails long but unpainted, the cuticles fraying. 'She thought of him as her last chance at love,' she murmured, after a moment. 'She didn't tell me who he was, or what he did—none of that—but she did say that she wanted to leave this world knowing that someone besides her own children would miss her.'

'She had such a low opinion of Papa?' There was no reproof any longer in Vicky's voice, as if he had, in the space of just a couple of minutes, resigned himself to what his mother had done. As if he and his sister were speaking no longer of their own parents but of some stranger. Detached, clinical. Meera reached out a hand and patted his shoulder. She was about to say something when they heard a sound below, a car pulling up outside the gate.

It stopped, and a man got out to open the gate before getting back in the car and driving in.

Vicky froze. 'That's the car! That's him, that's the car I saw that day. The man who was visiting Mummy.'

Meera peered down, watching as the car stopped and the man got out again, to go and close the gate. Even as he did so, the front door of the house opened. A bar of yellow light shone onto the lawn, with a stocky figure silhouetted against it. A moment, another—and the bar widened into a rectangle. The blackness of the figure filled it. Another followed, and another. Papa, leading the trio, saw the car and the man, and called out, 'Pradeep! I thought you weren't in town.'

They had reached each other by now, Pradeep putting an arm around Papa's shoulders, saying who knew what words of consolation. Meera and Vicky watched from above as the two men finally drew apart and Papa said something. At this distance, they could not hear his words, but from the hand gesturing towards the front door, and then pointing off to the left, where the largest room at the end had been used as a temporary prayer room, it seemed that Papa was telling his guest to go in and sit down. He had not made it for the funeral, or for the prayer meeting that had followed, but he was here now, ready with his sympathy.

Meera looked up at Vicky, her eyes worried. 'Are you sure? Pradeep Uncle has been such a good friend to both of them.'

'It's him. I recognize the car. You don't see that shade of blue in Altos, it has to have been specially painted.'

'Pradeep Uncle,' she murmured, looking back down again. She looked dazed.

Downstairs, Papa and his two friends had drifted out onto the lawn. Strolling aimlessly, one of them with an arm slung around the shoulders of another while the third walked a step behind. Snatches of conversation drifted up to the two people standing on the balcony.

Someone was talking about an offer. A road trip, into the hills. Simla. Thanedhar. Beyond. 'This is the right time to go, too.' And it would be such a relief to get away from all this. 'Delhi is so hot right now. You need it.' The other man was nodding, adding something in a lower voice. Something about a stopover at Chandigarh, and a visit to an old friend. 'Do you remember—' and the conversation was drifting off into reminiscences of college life and long-ago friends. Someone laughed. Someone else said, sharply, 'Shh!'

Meera turned and walked away from the balcony. Vicky followed her to the door, where she paused. 'She didn't tell Papa, Vicky,' she said. 'Don't tell me you wonder why.'

There was silence, except for the clicking of a gecko on a wall. And, somewhere in a far corner of the neighbourhood, the shrill whistle of the watchman.

'And Pradeep Uncle? Did she tell him? You never said.'

Meera nodded. 'She did. She said the man knew. Because she thought she owed it to him.'

For almost a minute, Vicky stood still, staring into space, his gaze wandering across the rooftops, the night sky lit up with so much ambient light that it hardly seemed like night any more. 'But she didn't tell Papa,' he said finally.

Meera said nothing, and after a moment, he shrugged. 'I thought she wronged Papa. Now I'm not sure who wronged who.'

From the lawn below came the muffled sound of laughter, quickly suppressed, followed by conversation.

'Let's go down,' Meera said. 'Pradeep Uncle will be all alone. We should go say hello.'

Vicky raised an eyebrow. 'You aren't going to—?'

'What? Confront him?' She shook her head, a sardonic smile briefly touching her lips. 'Of course not. What's the point, now? And if he was the one who relieved her loneliness and brought Mummy some joy in her last days… I can't hate him for that, Vicky. Let's go, shall we?'

They went down the stairs, their footsteps echoing down the stairwell. Outside, on the lawn, one of Papa's friends began talking of a long-ago trip to Mussoorie, and of what a fabulous time they had had.

Poppies in the Snow

AN OLD MAN once told me that the stream from which we draw water comes from high up in the mountains, behind the deodars. Above the tree line. From the snows. 'If you climb up, Iqbal,' he had said, squinting up at the distant peaks, 'you will see it. You will see snow melt into water. The purest water, clear as crystal, fresh and sweet. You could kill for water like that.'

I was not even ten then. It was a simpler world, a quieter one. A world where cold, clear water could be thought of in such poetic terms. Even then, I had thought him odd, senile. Who would kill for water?

I know better now. I have seen men kill for water. And not just for water, but for less. A word misheard, an action misunderstood. A matter of opinion, a sudden rage. For the pleasure of killing. For the exhilaration of knowing that one had lessened the enemy's numbers by one. As if, where there were thousands waiting, one would make a difference.

If you follow our stream up till the big brown boulder with its crown of lichens, you will see the stream split. A smaller branch, faster and narrower, goes off to the west. A couple of minutes' walk, and you come to a meadow on the mountainside. In the summer, it is beautiful. The grass is green, and there are poppies everywhere. Vivid red, their petals so thin that if you hold one up to the light, you can see the sun through it. Bright flowers, vibrant. Short-lived.

It was here that Mohsin died. In this meadow, his blood sprayed all across. It was autumn. There was not a poppy in the meadow, but it was red. Red with Mohsin's blood.

Three months, that is all it has been. Three months, in which even the brown of the grass has withered away. The ground is covered, right now, with perhaps six inches of snow. It has been snowing, off and on, for the past two days. The stream, where it slows down in the meadow, is rimmed with ice. There is utter silence here, the brooding shadows of the deodars behind me dark, grim.

The sky above is the colour of steel. There is more snow coming. I shoulder my gun, feel its weight on my arm. A comforting weight, a burden I am grateful for. It is an AK-47, once Mohsin's, now mine. It has killed men. Perhaps half a dozen, perhaps more. Sometimes when you fire into the dark, you hear a scream as the bullet strikes home, but you cannot tell if a man has been merely hurt or if he has died. And you are too busy to go and look. Too busy trying to stay alive, too busy trying to kill others.

* * *

I have collected an armload of firewood, enough for the next couple of days. Tied in a bundle with rope around it, the load bangs against my hip as I straighten, readying to return.

Just as I turn, I hear a voice behind me. A hushed voice, but echoing in the stillness of the woods nearby. 'Iqbal!'

Even without turning, even though it has been a while, I know who it is. I set my load down on a convenient rock. Sling the gun off my shoulder and around.

'It's I,' Aslam says as he emerges from the trees. 'Only I, Iqbal. Don't point that at me.' He is as old as I, perhaps a year or two older. Certainly no more than thirty. Tall, grey-eyed, his cheeks gaunt under a sprinkling of stubble. The dirty brown phiran swishing about his knees cannot hide his thinness. A thinness not of lean strength, but of having to do without. He has been living off the land.

One of them, I remind myself.

I do not remember the first time I saw Aslam; it must have been at least three years back, perhaps more. Mohsin had brought him to me, his face bright and eager. 'This is Aslam,' he had said. 'The very best. My brother who was not born to my parents, are you not, Aslam?' They had stood there, Mohsin's arm slung loosely across Aslam's shoulder, both wearing grins of matching eagerness.

I had stared, taken aback, while Mohsin had called for kahwa and had whispered something about cooking something decent for dinner, not our usual thrown-together meal of haaq and rice. That night, after we had eaten, we sat around. Drinking kahwa, warming our hands on our individual kaangris, filled with embers from the kitchen fire. And listening to Aslam. He spoke even more eloquently and with more fervour than Mohsin. He entranced us, convinced us. If I close my eyes, I can still see that scene. The light from the lantern dancing on the walls, on Aslam's thin, animated face. On Mohsin's face, wearing a look of pride, the pride of a parent when a child does him proud.

Aslam is less animated now. His eyes do not shine so vividly, and his smile is very brief: a gesture of greeting, of recognition. Momentary.

I do not say anything, just nod.

He glances again at my gun. I turn it away, swinging it

back onto my shoulder. We stand there in the snow, facing each other.

'It has changed,' he says after a while. The silence has stretched, long enough for me to be able to feel the chill of damp cloth around my ankles, the cold metal of the gun barrel where my fingers brush against it. 'Everything has changed,' he adds, as if to clarify.

'What did you expect? And it isn't as if it has changed suddenly. It had changed even before you left. You've been gone three months. That is long enough here.'

I see a flicker of something in his eyes. Resentment? Remorse? I cannot tell.

I want him to leave. I want to leave. I don't want to stand here, talking to this man. He reminds me of Mohsin, and of how Mohsin died. The wounds are too fresh. One memory, one moment that I know will never return, and it is enough to make my heart clench.

When I do not speak, Aslam sighs. 'Even if it has changed, surely you do not doubt me? I was Mohsin's best friend. His brother, he called me.' He glances about, at the line of deodars, and then off to his left, where the meadow falls away, to a view that is all white and shades of grey: the mountains, streaked with white, the valleys and folds and belts of trees dark.

'What are you doing here?' he asks, when I do not reply.

I shrug. 'Gathering wood.'

He looks sceptical. Who would not? There are woods closer home. But he knows, as do I—as do all of us—that there is something about this meadow that sets it apart. It is a vantage point like none other. From here, you can look out all across the valley, from the morel-shaped cliff to the east, right down, along the highway that leads to

Baramullah, off to the west. You can see everything from here. On a clear day, Mohsin once said, you can even imagine the shadow of Srinagar.

'Have you been looking about?' Aslam asks, his voice low. As if anybody can hear him here. 'Is that why you're carrying the gun?'

'I never venture out this far without my gun,' I say.

He looks out, about. Across the mountains. 'The Indian Army is gone,' he says, untruthfully. 'We flushed out every single one of them. Bombed them, gunned them down. Do you remember that ambush, that convoy? One jonga after another, and those Shaktimans? So many of them, and we took them all down.' He is not looking at me, his eyes are far away, his gaze resting on some long-ago laurels. 'Mohsin was there too,' he murmurs. 'What a fine man he was.'

* * *

That was in the early days. The fervour, the anger, the disillusionment had been building up over the years into a storm waiting to burst. We had inherited it from our fathers and mothers, and their parents before them. Back how far, we did not know. But the cry was universal: the only way Kashmir was to survive, the only way we could continue, was if we were free. There had been resentment, festering against India, since well before Partition. India wants us only for what it can get, we heard our forefathers say. The beauty of Kashmir, the revenues from tourism. Handicrafts. Saffron, dry fruit, pashmina. Most important of all, a barrier against China and Pakistan. That is why India needs us. For its own selfish reasons, not because they have any need of the Kashmiri people. Not because they love us or feel we are part of India.

Pakistan will be better, many said. They have more of an affinity for Kashmir. And they can offer us an Islamic state. We will be welcomed with open arms.

It took time, wisdom, more disillusionment, to realize that that wasn't the case, either. That Pakistan was as bad as India. Perhaps worse. Azadi, freedom, was what we really needed. Freedom for Kashmir, not affiliation to either of these two countries we found ourselves sandwiched between.

'It is the mujahideen who will bring us freedom,' Mohsin had said. He was—what? Twenty-five? I don't remember how long back that was. But I do remember the light in his eyes, the fierceness in his face, the way his hands clenched unconsciously into fists when he spoke of the mujahideen and what they would do for us, for Kashmir. He was not one of them. He was just a villager, a poor man who survived because he worked desperately hard, doing everything from herding sheep to looking after his vegetable patch, his terraced fields of rice, his little orchard of hard, sour apples.

I do not know how he got to know the mujahideen— whether they made the overture, or he did—but it was Mohsin who told us about them. Brought Aslam to us.

From the very beginning, too, it was Mohsin who was the most ardent of us all. Even I had my reservations. I, who was the most loyal to Mohsin, who would have stood by him no matter what. Who *did* stand by him. Our altercations, our disagreements, happened in private.

I would ask him what made him think the mujahideen were any better than the Indians or the Pakistanis. Why did he trust them? Why did he think they would be able to do what so many people, in so many years, had not succeeded in achieving?

He could never quite convince me, though he said something about people who were willing to lay down their lives for the cause.

In any case, I was just one voice of dissent. Who would listen to me? Mohsin, least of all. He was smugly comfortable in the knowledge that I would not abandon him, would not even voice my objections in public.

Until the day Azra spoke up.

* * *

'Do you remember,' says Aslam, 'before—before'—he gropes awkwardly for a word, a phrase that will be the truth but will neither humiliate him nor point a finger at us. Before *you switched sides*, he could say. Before *you decided you had had enough*. Before *you realized the mujahideen were the mere vanguard*.

He stops, swallows. 'Mohsin and I had gone to Hazratbal.'

Yes, I remember. I had not gone, of course. Only Aslam and Mohsin, to that huge, white-domed mosque in Srinagar where they say the Prophet's hair is kept. They had gone to Srinagar for something else, something so secret Mohsin had not even told me, before he went. It was only later, much later, that he had confessed: they had gone to meet some mujahideen. Not at the masjid, but nearby. To discuss attacks they were planning, to talk about support the mujahideen needed. Why in Srinagar, I had asked. We don't live anywhere near Srinagar. What support could we provide to mujahideen planning anything in Srinagar? And if they had meant here, in our mountains, then why meet in Srinagar?

'Idiot,' Mohsin had said, but with affection. 'You don't understand, do you? They think highly of me. They want the men higher up to get to know me.' I could see the pride in him, the triumph. 'Someday, soon, perhaps, they will ask me to do something really important for them.'

But what they asked was not what we had become used to. They did not ask, any longer, for us to merely shelter their men. They did not ask that we hide them and lie to the Indian Army about their whereabouts. They did not ask us only for food and water—which we had been giving them, without any money in exchange, just out of a sense of patriotic pride, a feeling that we were helping in the struggle for freedom.

They did not ask us. They demanded it. They demanded more food. They demanded the last of our firewood, the last grains of rice, the last few walnuts, the last sheep. Worst of all, they began demanding our women. Men on a quest that will end their lives need women, they said. They need relief, they need the comfort of—well, they called it love, but what love can a woman give who is being forced?

It had begun slowly, the gradual realization that these were not just Kashmiri men fighting for Kashmiri freedom, but insurgents from across the border. Men who did not see us as kin. Men who were here fighting not for our liberation—as Aslam had assured us he and his men were— but men fighting to get rid of the Indian Army so that Kashmir could be joined to Pakistan.

In the beginning, it was resentment. Resentment, because they were taking away from us what we needed so desperately ourselves. People grumbled, but gave what they could. Whimpered when they could not and it was snatched from them. Occasionally, when what was demanded was simply impossible, there would be murmurs.

Azra had shouted at them as they took away her last sack of rice: 'And what will we eat, eh? What will we eat?' To which they had laughed. One had suggested something obscene. And when she had lunged at him, too angry to think, he had kicked her in the stomach. Again and again and again, until she was spewing blood. She was six months pregnant, and she gave birth to her dead baby there and then, in the freezing mud of the village lane. Only when the mujahideen had left the village, dragging away more sheep, more sacks, one entire cartload of firewood—had we emerged and gone to Azra's aid.

The women had kept vigil all night about her bed. The men had clustered together in one house.

There was confusion, hurt. Betrayal. Fear. But most of all, there was rage. This was not what we had imagined. This was not what we had been promised. The old men spoke up, questioning. Was this the freedom they were going to give us? At this cost? Would any of us remain alive to savour that freedom? Or would they kill us all, the way they had killed Azra's unborn child?

Mohsin tried to quell their fears, tried to tell them it would pass. Perhaps he was trying, desperately, to believe that himself. Perhaps he knew—and I thought I saw that knowledge in his eyes—that it was a forlorn hope.

Sometime during that long night, Azra died.

* * *

'What about Hazratbal?' I ask. If he wants to talk, so be it. I can wait.

He stares at me. Recognizes, perhaps, the anger in my voice. I am too tired to keep up the pretence, even of indifference, any longer. Mohsin is dead and gone, and Aslam—the Aslam Mohsin had trusted so deeply, even with his own life—has gone, too. Even though I never had liked him, had never got over my suspicion that he would be more traitor than patriot.

He shakes his head. 'No. Nothing.'

I shrug. 'Well, then. I will go. I have to get home.'

'Wait.' He reaches out a hand to stop me. 'Is—is it really—like this?' He gestures towards my gun, which I have not put down for an instant all this while. 'Do all of you carry guns? All?'

'Where have you been all this while?' I snap back. 'Have you been asleep?'

He frowns. 'You have no idea how things have been for me, caught between you lot and'—he fumbles again, actually flushes—'them.'

'Why? Do they not pay you well to pimp for them?'

I could have said *steal*. I could have said *kill*. I could have said *thrash*. Or whatever. But what remains in my mind is that memory of the day I entered the house to find Aslam and Mohsin in the middle of an argument. They did not see me come in, they were on the floor above, where we lived. I came into the cowshed below, putting down a load of hay near the trough. The cows, tethered by their ropes moved restlessly about, distressed by the loud voices coming down the wide wooden staircase with its shallow steps. I did not climb up, to see for myself or to intervene. I simply stood there, and listened.

It was about a woman.

Aslam was asking for a woman. No, not asking, demanding. Not for himself, he was shouting. *Not for himself*. For Riaz, he was saying. Riaz. Riaz was the leader of the gang of militants who had set up camp in the woods on the hill opposite. A tall man, broad and prematurely grey, with a bulbous nose and an air of menace about him. He, I remembered, was the one who had kicked Azra. Not just a very dangerous man, but one with no soul, either. A woman who was taken to Riaz would not come away alive. Even if she breathed, she would not be alive.

'What do you want?' I had heard Aslam saying, his voice strident. 'For Riaz to attack? Do you know what will happen? Have you any idea—'

The rest had been drowned out. In curses, in shouting, in the sound of a scuffle, of blows. Then, of weeping. Aslam's, loud howls of pain. Mohsin's, a low keening that sounded to my stricken ears more like a dirge, a wail of mourning. As if he were crying for what might have been.

Five minutes later, and Aslam had gone: I heard him mutter a quick—and ironic—khuda hafiz. Then the door swung open on rusty hinges, and thudded shut. Five minutes after that, I poked my head out of the lower door—the cattle door, we called it—and watched as Mohsin walked slowly away, his head bowed. As if life had become too heavy a burden to bear.

* * *

Aslam scowls at me. I can see a nerve twitch in one cheek. He used to be handsome once upon a time, now he is not. I have never seen him look so gaunt, so haggard. As if he has not been eating. More than that, there is the look in his eyes. Haunted. Hunted.

Yes, I think. Hunted, he is. Possibly haunted, too. Haunted by the ghost of Azra. Of Zareen and Gulrukh and Mariam and the other girls and women he helped Riaz carry off.

'I do not pimp,' he says. His words lack conviction.

'You are not paid for it?' I am too bitter, too angry, to realize that it could be dangerous to goad a man like this.

To my astonishment, instead of hitting me, Aslam slumps against a half-fallen tree trunk, leaning back against it as if his legs were no longer capable of holding him up. For the briefest of moments, I feel pity for him. He is like us, too. Somewhat. A poor villager, who got into the wrong company, as old Abdul would have said. Led astray as a young man. Young, impressionable, easily carried away by dreams of glory and honour and a Kashmir we had all imagined could some day come true, if all of us only worked a little harder...

But Aslam did not have something we did: we had consciences. We had ties. Zareen may not have been kin, no blood relative of most of the villagers, but when she was caught and raped—in full daylight, while she was out gathering firewood—the entire village's honour was tainted. When, two days later, Gulrukh was carried off almost from her doorstep, panic set in. And when Aslam came to Mohsin, telling him that Riaz had told him to fetch Mariam—Mariam, apple-cheeked and blue-eyed, fresh and pretty as an orchard in bloom—that panic changed to anger.

The elders gathered in one house. Those of us who could find space, squeezed into the adjoining rooms. Those who could not, stood outside.

They talked through much of the evening. We listened, waiting with bated breath. There were one or two—the loners, those with no women to lose, no valuables to be carried away—who tried to advocate Riaz. Their attempts to brush away the raping and the looting were feeble. This was jihad, they said. A holy war. Things happened in war that would not happen in peacetime. Someday all would be well.

The elders came to a decision after hours of deliberation. The next morning, a small delegation set off from the village, with Mohsin at its head. He had insisted on being part of it, because—as he told me, so many times over the next few weeks—'I am the one who brought Aslam here. If it hadn't been for me, this would never have happened.' Mohsin could be as merciless when it came to punishing himself as he was when going into battle with an enemy.

And now everybody—or everybody with a say, everybody who mattered—had agreed that it was time to put an end to this. They went to the local Indian Army camp, to the commander, and asked for help. Help us fight the insurgents. Train us. Give us guns.

It would not happen overnight, of course. Even we knew that. The Indian Army were, as was to be expected, cautious. They knew full well that we had sheltered militants, had helped them, these past couple of years. Even though Mohsin and the others told them what had caused the change of heart, why we wanted to change sides, the commander did not make a commitment right then. Give me time, he said. I have to talk to my superiors.

And while that little delegation was away, Riaz and his men swooped down on the village and raided it, taking away more of what they wanted. Including Mariam. We could hear her mother's screams echoing through the alley in which their house stood, long after the militants had gone.

Three days later, the army came.

It was not as if we had not seen AK-47s before. They were legendary, they were familiar. Even if we had never held one before, we knew what it was. But there was a sense of awe in handling one of them. In training, in practising, in learning how to clean, and load, and aim, and fire. In the realization that if—*when*—Riaz and his men came around the next time, we would be ready to meet them.

Muzammil was the first to be killed. Some said he was Riaz's nephew. Others said no, he was a cousin. At any rate, he was dear to Riaz, and one of those whose absence would be felt.

It would also be avenged.

That was what started off the war, because war it was. Riaz was not going to forgive us so easily for what he thought of as betrayal. We had turned against him, even if his pushing us to the brink had been the cause. He attacked us, pummelled us. Carried off our livestock as it grazed, set fire to the houses on the fringes of the village.

But we had help. The army was now there, helping us. And we were helping ourselves, too. Now we fought back, and for every villager Riaz and his men killed, we inflicted some damage on them. It may only be a graze, a broken leg, or a furrow dug through a scalp, but it was there, a reminder that we were not going to let them ride roughshod over us.

Then, one night, when the entire village was asleep, I woke to hear the low murmur of voices. Not in the house, but on the slope above, where the old walnut tree stood. I would have turned over and gone back to sleep, had I not realized then that Mohsin was missing. When you live in such close proximity to a man, when he becomes a part of you, his very breathing a part of your life, of the space you inhabit—then your recognition of his absence becomes instinctive. I did not have to look around, did not have to whisper his name into the dark. I just knew he was not there.

* * *

Three months. Three months it has been, and I still remember that night. Still remember the chill as I stepped out. Not even winter yet, but when does the cold ever really go away in this land of ours? I remember creeping out, one hand resting on the wooden wall of the house, the other clutching the gun—Mohsin had forgotten it—or had he left it behind, deliberately?—which stood always on the inside of the door, ready to be snatched up.

I remember climbing up the slope to the walnut tree, and realizing even as I climbed that the voices had fallen silent. Had they heard me coming? Were they lying in wait for me? A horrible thought came into my mind: was it possible that Mohsin had switched back? Had Riaz and Aslam, between them, seduced him back to the side of the militants? Why had Mohsin come out this late at night to talk to someone? It was clandestine. Anything clandestine is certain to be wrong. In some way or the other.

When I reached the walnut tree, they were gone. It was still, silent. The stars glittering in the deep blue-black of the sky above. The moonlight, washing over the trees, the sleeping village.

And then the shot rang out. Not very far, away to the west.

Mohsin had left his gun behind. His gun was with me, hanging from my shoulder.

I ran, ran towards the west. Gasping, sobbing, telling myself that there was another explanation for the shot. Perhaps there was another, another villager, who had gone with Mohsin. A man who bore a gun. And they had encountered a militant and the other man had fired...

When I burst into the clearing, the smell of that shot still hung in the air. And mingled with it was the metallic smell of blood.

Here.

I do not know how or when I made my way back to the village and fetched help. I remember looking down at him, and wondering how a man could have bled so much. I had seen my share of corpses—of people who had died violently—but it is different with someone you have known. Someone you have known the way I had known Mohsin, so deeply, so dearly.

There is no sign of him here now. No stench of blood, not a single crimson splash. Not even under the snow that blankets this meadow.

I look up at Aslam.

'You know,' I say, 'I did not realize that you were not there for his funeral. Or that I did not see you after that night.'

He looks uncomfortable. He mumbles something. About hostility, about people in the village being too ready with their guns.

'Not when it comes to you,' I point out. 'Even though you brought the insurgents to our doorstep, we have never harmed you.' True, that. Old Abdul had said, 'He is a misguided child, that one. Has he ever killed one of us? Stolen from us? Until he does that, perhaps we can let him be. There is no virtue in turning as cold-blooded as them.'

So Aslam had still come and gone. But his visits had become infrequent, and very brief: even he realized he was walking a tightrope here. He had to run the gauntlet of stares, or muttered imprecations. Even, one day, a maddened assault by Gulrukh's father, who had come running after Aslam, a willow whip in one hand, a heavy stone in the other. The stone had gone wide of its mark, but the whip had slashed at Aslam, again and again.

But I never saw Aslam, not even a glimpse of him, after the night Mohsin died. Until today.

He shrugs. 'It is dangerous,' he insists.

'I should be going,' I say. I steady my gun. 'Riaz was killed, did you know? A week back.'

He nods. He's looking down at the ground, not at me. I can sense the wariness in him. 'Of course I know.' I can barely hear him, his voice is so low. If the world were not so silent right now, if the snow did not blanket everything and muffle every sound, I would not have heard him.

'After Riaz was killed,' I add, 'Mariam escaped. She came home.'

His head jerks up at that. There is dread in those grey eyes of his.

'Yes.' I swallow. I have to be careful how I say this. I cannot make a mistake. It must be correct. 'Yes, she came back. And she told me what happened that night, three months back. She said there had been rumours that Riaz had sent you, to bring another woman. And you did not have the courage to refuse. So you came to Mohsin, to ask him. Did you really think he would agree? Was that what you thought of Mohsin?'

'Iqbal—'

'Mariam heard the rumours, you know. She told me.'

'Iqbal, believe me—'

'And she was there, in the next room, when you came to meet Riaz. You told him the truth. You had killed Mohsin.'

He is looking around frantically now, searching for the gun he probably has close by. Not close enough, though. Not close enough.

'You have been living by yourself in that cave above the fallen deodar, isn't it? Mariam told me. Just two minutes from here. What did you tell Mohsin that night? That you wanted him to come to the cave, so that the two of you could discuss it?'

He shakes his head. There is an air of weariness about him. 'I told him to let it be,' he said. 'He was not listening, anyway. I told him we would part ways, but we would part as brothers. Brothers. Do you hear, Iqbal? Brothers.' His voice rises. I can hear the panic in it. He knows that I am not just suspicious. I know.

'No,' I say. My hand, under cover of the shawl that wraps about my head and hangs down the side of my phiran, reaches for the trigger. 'Mariam told me something else, too. That she later learnt the truth. Riaz had not sent you to Mohsin that night. You had come of your own accord. You wanted a woman for yourself.'

He pales. I swing the gun forward. 'For me,' I say, as I pull the trigger. 'You came for me.'

Aslam's body jerks, again and again, as the bullets strike. My aim is good. I have practised long and hard, especially in this last week. And he was standing close. Too close for me to miss.

I have avenged my husband.

Author's Note: In many Kashmiri villages, the dream of Azadi had originally encouraged villagers to help insurgents. Later, with increasingly unreasonable demands from the insurgents, the villagers turned to the Indian Army for help, and have since been trained in the use of firearms. Village Defence Committees (VDCs) have been set up, and some—like the twin villages of Kulali and Marrah (in Poonch district) even have all-women VDCs. (Iqbal, meaning 'prosperity' or 'good fortune' is a name used interchangeably for both male and female).

Acknowledgements

THIS BOOK—AND, truth to tell, all my writing—would probably not have come about if it had not been for the two people to whom this book is dedicated. For one, my mother, Muriel Liddle, who was my first teacher (quite literally, too, since there was no proper school in the town where we lived when I should've been in nursery). It was Mama who instilled in me a love for the language, and who told me stories and anecdotes of her family, even from several generations back. Some of those stories, now almost lore in our family, have made their way into this collection, even if only thinly disguised.

Swapna Dutta, for many years now an eminent author and translator, was my mother's best friend in college—and an inspiration for me, in all the years I have known her. It was she whose example I followed, and it was she who gave me my first tips on writing. To Swapna Aunty, and to Mama, I can never be grateful enough.

Several other people have, in some way or another, contributed to this book. Katharina Finke, who, while doing research for her book, *Mit dem Herzen einer Tigerin* (*With the Heart of a Tiger*), took me into the heart of Mewat and exposed me to the horrors of bride trafficking. My editor, Renuka Chatterjee, who saw the potential in these stories, and honed them. And, as always, my husband Tarun, who was my first reader in each instance: patient, supportive, critical.

Thank you, all.